Liv at the End of the World
K.H. Walters

Copyright © 2024 Katherine Walters
All rights reserved.
No part of this book may be reproduced or transmitted by any means, except as permitted by UK copyright law or the author. For licensing requests, please contact the author at: kathywalterswrites@gmail.com

A note on content: Some scenes in this book may be upsetting for some readers. A non-exhaustive list of potentially upsetting content may be reviewed at my website: https://kathywritesfantasy.wordpress.com/content-warnings

For my dad, Ian, who is there for me always, and who is one of the people I would want to spend the end of the world with

Contents

Sunday – Old age and aliens 11

The pillow fort 20

Monday – A trip to the office 29

Dreams and middle names 43

Tuesday – Roommates 48

Our little gods 60

Wednesday – The most important job 67

The ocean 78

Thursday – The Yorkshire pudding of fears 91

Again? Again! 105

Friday – The Eulogy 114

Friday – Not about the food 120

The wrong bin 129

Saturday – Power cuts 145

Sunday – Bumblebee 158

The good days 164

Sunday – The decision 173

Sunday – The end 182

Author's note

This book came to me in a dream. Given the subject matter, I am sure you can imagine what a fun night's sleep that was! The dream went like this: aliens announced they needed to destroy the earth because we were all carrying a deadly disease. Then I looked at myself and saw that I did, indeed, have a deadly disease. But we all just decided to have a big party and enjoy our final hours.

I woke up and told my fiancé and he said it would make a cool book. I agreed. After all, I'm a comedy writer and what's funnier than the end of the world and the deaths of everyone we know and love.

After that, it was a race against the clock. When you're writing a book about the destruction of Earth, you always kind of hope that the world won't actually end before you publish, because that would be a pretty big spoiler. I have been crossing my fingers intently since I started writing this one. I haven't even been able to look at the news.

If you're reading this, we made it, or there's an afterlife. Either way, we win!

Sunday – Old age and aliens

This is quite a happy story, except for the fact that it ends with the destruction of Earth.

If you'd asked me a few months ago how I thought the world would end, I would definitely have gone with nuclear winter. Not that I wanted to live through a nuclear war, of course, but any time I went on the internet to try and look for cute dog videos, I always ended up down a rabbit hole of the reasons we are approaching World War III. Honestly, the fact that aliens were going to do it was a welcome surprise. A bit like how if you have to get murdered, you'd probably prefer it was a serial killer instead of your mum.

The announcement came on a Sunday, rudely interrupting the quiz show I was watching.

'Oh, um,' said a woman in a purple top with a name tag that read "Nicole." 'I don't know any of them.'

'No?' said the quiz show host. 'Nothing springing to mind? Why don't you try guessing something?'

Nicole smiled wanly. 'I think I'll have to. I'll guess Æthelred the Unready for the second one down, then.' She was absolutely astounded when her "guess" turned out to be correct.

I was understandably incensed. If there was one thing I hated more than anything, it was when people wouldn't admit they actually knew the answer on quiz shows. I instinctively got out my phone to message my sister Bex. Then my thumb froze on the screen. I stared at her name in my contacts.

'What a lucky *guess,* "Nicole!"' I yelled. I reached for my glass of wine. 'Look at this, Nicole. You're driving me to drink!'

And that was it. The very last normal moment of my life. I can't help wonder how many people were doing the same thing I was. There were lots of reasons to shout at the telly. My schoolfriend, Eva, liked to watch horror movies, so she could tell the characters what idiots they were. And my dad used the best swear words to berate football players when I was growing up. I knew they were good ones because I'd gotten a week's worth of detentions for directing just one of them at a teacher. I liked thinking of all the other people doing exactly the same thing as me. Like we were one big hive mind processing the bad news together. It made me feel less alone.

The message announcing the end began with the high pitched squeal of audio feedback. This was fair enough, if you asked the aliens, because they hadn't used Earth's tannoy system in over a million years. It was bound to be rusty. What did we expect?

A terrifying voice began, '*Sssssidefannnnnpphhh.*' At least, that was how Shine would tell me it should be transcribed in earth characters the following day. 'You don't have a proper way to denote the unglottian micro-vowel,' he would lament. But I'm getting ahead of myself. Pretend I didn't say anything about Shine yet.

Luckily, the earth's tannoy had simultaneous interpretation. Unluckily, this was *also* broken. So after a few seconds of gobbledygook which Shine assured me were particularly shocking alien curse words, another voice joined the first.

'Good morning Earth beings!' This voice was far more upbeat, but had some kind of accent. Specifically, it had the kind of accent that made it sound like the DJ at my Aunt Mary's wedding as we were closing in on midnight and he was closing in on his twelfth pint. 'I'm Luna the Eighty-First and I'm here to be an interpreter for my good friend Sol the First of the SSSSSSSiiiisssssttttm. I am sure you all know them as Deputy Prime Minister of the Known-Universe. Give me a second to hold for applause.'

I'm not sure how it went down elsewhere in the world, but here in the UK we do what we're told when it comes to clapping for things. Uncertain

14.

applause sounded about my neighbourhood. I heard next-door's teenage daughter, Lily, give it a good, 'Woooo!'

On the telly, Nicole got a question wrong and it was looking likely she'd be going home. I took a sip of my wine and smiled smugly.

Sol the First, Deputy Prime Minister of the Known-Universe, started to talk again. All the consonants were giving me a headache, but at least there was Luna the Eighty-First to interpret now. 'Earth beings, we are pleased to announce that you are not alone in the universe. In fact, there are many different and far more intelligent life forms out here, isn't that great? Sadly, you will never get to meet any of them.' She was doing ever such a good job keeping up with Sol. Not like some of those interpreters on the telly who seemed to stumble over bits and miss them out. Mind, how would I know if she was getting anything wrong? It's not like I spoke alien. I poured myself another glass. 'It has come to our attention that you are all super spreaders of a deadly disease. Uhoh!'

I didn't feel poorly. I put a hand to my forehead to check if I was hot. Admittedly I'd had a bit of a sore throat when I'd woken up, but I'd thought that was just because it was a cold night. Surely the whole world wasn't dying of the common cold. Although, wasn't that what happened in The War of the

15.

Worlds? Or was that the aliens who died? Either way, I supposed it wouldn't be good for Luna and Sol and all their little pals.

Through the paper-thin wall I heard Lily's dad, Max, say, 'What the actual f-?'

'That's right! You are carrying what we believe in your tongue is known as "the old age."'

'How dare they call me old!' shouted Max.

'Calm down, love,' Max's wife, Anna, whispered. 'I'm sure they weren't talking about you.'

Still sounding drunk and chipper, Luna interpreted, 'I am getting from the feedback that old age might have been a "culturally insensitive" term. Whoopsie! Apparently you don't have a word for this disease at all because you consider it part of the normal cycle of life. Fancy that! You have no idea that one of your ancestors from almost three million years ago caught something nasty from eating the wrong insect. So now every single one of you has a highly infectious disease that cuts your life span down to ten percent. That's right! If we could cure this disease, the average human could live between seven hundred and a thousand years.'

The aliens left a pause there for the whole world to mumble in amazement.

'Anyway. We can't cure the disease. So we're going to have to blow up the planet instead.'

16.

It seemed like everyone and their grandmother had something to say about that. For instance, Max my neighbour said, 'You f-ing a-holes! How f-ing dare you!' and then he immediately said, 'Sorry, alien overlords. Please spare us.' Whereas his grandmother let out a string of expletives so obscene that I can't even find a way to censor them.

'We understand that this must be a very difficult time for you all,' the alien went on in the same tone my first boss had used when he made me redundant after I'd worked there three days. 'Unfortunately, we are unable to reverse the decision at this time. We do try, wherever possible, to avoid an extinction event such as this one, but the risk of your disease spreading through the rest of the universe is, say it with me, "too great to take".' No one said it with her. There was some rustling then she added, 'Sorry, I'm getting feedback that you don't know that holo-show.'

'We'll stop space travel!' Max was wailing. I hadn't known he had an in with Nasa. 'We'll just stay in our little planet! I promise!'

I'd never find out how, among all the millions of voices presumably pleading for their lives in that moment, the aliens heard my neighbour. But hear him they did. I knew this because they said, 'We hear you, Max Smith. And we thank you for your representation of the planet Earth at this time.

However, it is our experience that whenever a group of sentient beings promises to stay put in order to not spread a deadly disease through the known-universe, they never fulfil that promise. We're looking at you Grektok of the Nineth System. Oh wait, none of you can hear us, because you're all dead.' She chuckled. At least I think she chuckled. It sounded like someone shaking a jar of stale raisins under a waterfall. 'Sorry, a little intergalactic humour there.'

'How long do we have?' shouted Max, taking his new position as Representative of Earth very seriously.

'Great question, Max Smith, Representative of Earth!' said the cheerful voice. 'The Government of the Known-Universe has benevolently decided to give you time to say goodbye to your loved ones and live it up before it's all over. So get your party shoes ready because you have one week. You heard me, one full week before your tragic but inevitable deaths. You're welcome!'

If I was struggling to watch the quiz show over the sound of aliens announcing the end of the world, I had no chance once all the screaming and crying started. Max's chorus of 'Why? Why? Why?' might as well have been right in my earhole. I had a mind to knock on the wall like he did to me when I was practising the piano, but I didn't have the heart.

18.

'I can see you all need a little time to process, and that's ok. We'll do a farewell announcement in a week's time. Until then, I'll tell you what we always tell the planets we're culling for the safety of the universe. Think about what life really means to you and do as much of it as you can. Ta ra for now!'

I turned off the TV and sunk down into my chair. A melody of terrified screams continued to play through the neighbourhood, but I wasn't really listening to them. I felt numb. I wondered if it would click an hour or a day from now and I'd cry and throw lamps and all the things that everyone else was doing.

The truth was, although aliens planning to blow up the world was objectively shocking, I wasn't surprised. It felt like I'd been waiting for something like this to happen for a while now. I thought about when the screams died down and how all those people would be calling and texting loved ones. Planning to go sky diving or scuba diving or any other kind of extreme diving that people did to feel like they'd really lived. I didn't want to do anything other than sit in front of my TV and yell at quiz show contestants. There was no one left for me to call.

I thought about the decision I'd been struggling to make and how it should be inconsequential now.

It didn't feel that way. In fact, it felt like the most important thing I could do.

I got up, wine glass in hand, and made my way to the calendar.

'End of the world and I still can't find the bloody pen,' I grumbled to myself.

Eventually, I found one in the fridge. It was a bit cold but it still worked. I circled next Sunday, 9th March 2025. It was such a mundane day. Nothing at all special about it. There were so many meaningful days in March. The world could have ended on Pi day, for instance, and then we could have had a big farewell party with pie. Or it could have ended on St Patrick's day and we could have gone out roaring drunk and dressed in green. Wouldn't that be a sight to behold? All those lovely green suits floating into space in little bits. But no, the 9th was an empty box. I wrote "*END OF THE WORLD*" in it in block capitals, but even that didn't make me feel anything. I tried again. "*DECISION DAY.*"

Finally, I started to cry.

20.

The pillow fort

The history of Liv and Bex

If I told you I was the kind of person who made my whole personality about the fact that my mum abandoned me when I was a kid, would that explain some things?

Now, I should say that it wasn't just me she abandoned. There was my dad, of course. The man she had loved for a decade, which sounds a lot more impressive than ten years, and, to be honest, I'm rounding up. It was nine.

They met on the first day of university. My mum walked into the wrong lecture, late and hungover. After half an hour she raised her hand and said, 'Excuse me, I think you're teaching the wrong class. This is meant to be Intro to Rock.' That was the moment my dad fell in love. It was her audacity, he said. For this tiny little red-haired thing in an oversized AC-DC top to assume that a teacher and fifty other students would be the ones in the wrong.

The professor blinked at her. 'I'm sorry, this is the Rise and Fall of Napoleon. Have another look at your student schedule and you should be able to find the right classroom for your geology lecture.'

My mum stood up and wobbled a little because she wasn't actually hungover, it turned out. She was still drunk. 'Not that kind of rock!' she said. 'This kind!' And she proceeded to demonstrate her air guitar skills.

The professor was flummoxed. 'I'm quite certain we don't have a module about rock music here.'

That was the moment my mum realised she was at the wrong campus. It would later transpire she wasn't even in the right city. 'Oh,' she said, flopping back down in her chair. 'Well, I like Napoleon too.'

The professor probably should have kicked her out, but he didn't want the hassle. He carried on with his lecture as if nothing had happened.

After class, everyone was studiously avoiding her, except for my dad who rushed to her side. 'Do you need help getting home, love?'

'Where am I now?' She was still unsteady and he reached out to keep her upright. He said he did a lot of that over the years, holding her up when she struggled to stand.

'Sheffield,' he said.

'Sheffield?' She started counting on her fingers. 'Where's Sheffield?'

'Compared to where?'

'Edinburgh,' she slurred.

'Down,' said my dad. 'A lot down.'

22.

She snorted a laugh. 'What a crazy night!' And then she threw up all over his jumper.

The fact that my dad didn't care that she'd vomited on him was a sign that he was already head over heels. The fact that *she* didn't care that she'd thrown up on him, was a sign that she was not.

She confirmed that she did, in fact, need help getting home, and he agreed in a heartbeat. They went back to his flat first so that he could change his top. An unnecessary detour in her eyes, especially since his room was devoid of all signs of real music. No posters, no records, no Walkman, and his CDs were uninspiring to say the least.

'These are all boy bands.'

My dad shrugged. 'I like boy bands. They have catchy songs and they don't take themselves too seriously.'

Weirdly, that was when my mum started to fancy my dad. She said there was something really punk rock about a guy who wasn't afraid to admit he liked boybands. And then, all of a sudden, everything she had found boring about him before – the fact he changed one uninspiring jumper for another in the same colour, his floppy hair, the way he stood sort of hunched – became endearing instead.

He came with her to Edinburgh that day. Four hours there, four hours back, spending money he definitely didn't have, missing lectures he really shouldn't be missing. He didn't care about any of that because he got to kiss her when they said goodbye. It was the first of many kisses. It was also the gateway to an unplanned pregnancy at nineteen years old, a shotgun wedding and, eventually, us.

Yes, I said us. I wasn't just a me. I was almost thirty by the end of the world and I still couldn't imagine being pregnant with even one child. My mum, whose dream it was to be a rock star, was carrying two.

'There are two little people inside me?' she asked, when the doctor told her. 'At the same time?'

'That's usually how twins work, yes.'

'But I need confirmation that that's how *my* twins work.'

The doctor laughed and went to type up his notes.

'I wasn't joking!' she said, and he just laughed some more.

I was the older twin. That's important. Ask anybody. I had thirty whole minutes of being a spoilt only child, and then my sister interrupted the peace. Quite literally. I cried just enough to show everyone I was alive. My sister cried like she needed to alert the whole universe to her presence. The midwife said she'd never heard anything like it in all her twenty years on the job.

24.

My dad named us. I looked like an Olivia, she looked like a Rebecca. Liv and Bex.

My mum wasn't much of a baby person. She also wasn't much of a kid person. Had she stuck around long enough, I don't think she'd have been much of a teenager person either. It didn't matter, because my dad was all of those things.

Before mum left, Bex and I were normal children. We didn't have a psychic connection like you might expect of twins. This was proven over the course of several experiments. First, by Bex and I trying to read each other's minds and guess the right colours and words.

'Was it green, Bexy?'

'Oh, close but it was cerulean.'

Then by the kids at school kicking, poking and prodding me to see if Bex could feel it. She could not. However, *they* definitely felt something when she beat them up in retaliation.

Bex was always like that. The bold one. The fearless one. The one with "a bit of fire" as my mum used to say. I was quieter and meeker. I would have taken all that damage in my stride and never done anything about it. To be honest, I think I was just less than she was. And that was ok by me. I was always happy to be in Bex's shadow.

We were seven when my mum finally gave up on us all. My dad said it would have been better if she'd left without a word. Everything she did say was so selfish that he couldn't believe she was someone he loved. She'd never wanted to be a mother, she told us. She'd tried. God knows she'd tried to love us the way our dad did, but she wasn't as good as him. She wanted her own life. She wanted music back and wild nights and possibilities. There was another man, someone wiry thin and beautiful with long hair and tattoos. But the man wasn't important. We ought to forget the man really, because even without him we weren't what she wanted anymore.

And we'd probably all be better off without her.

'I can't even tell you apart for Christ's sake!' she said, with a self-deprecating little laugh that might have been charming if she wasn't ruining our whole lives.

'But we aren't even identical,' I wailed.

That didn't persuade her. She left anyway. I never got to find out if she made it as a rockstar. I asked Shine at some point near the end and he said I was better off not knowing. I wasn't sure if that was because she did have all her dreams come true without us, or because she didn't. I wasn't sure which would have been worse.

After my mum left, I asked a thousand quiet questions about why she didn't want me. Until I bored even myself with them, and realised it was better to keep it all inside. I distinctly remember Mrs Murs, my Year Four teacher, saying, 'Liv is a lovely little girl and we're all very happy that she's finally got over that little thing with her mum,' to my dad one parents' evening.

I hadn't got over it. I was just pretending really hard. Will you be embarrassed for me if I say that I never did? She hurt me right up until the end.

Bex, on the other hand, was a superhero. She jumped into everything two feet first. She was the centre of every social group at school. Adults loved her too. She was the kind of cheeky and disobedient that they had to pretend they didn't find amusing. I couldn't count the number of times one of our teachers had said, 'Bex, you can't say words like that,' or 'Bex, you're meant to be wearing the socks on your feet not as a headband,' or 'Bex, for the last time, the frogs have to stay in the pond.' Always in an exasperated voice. Always with a hand over their mouth to stop them from laughing.

She played Mary in the school nativity almost every year and if that's not a measure of a kid's social success, I don't know what is. Everyone told my dad, in hushed tones, that they couldn't believe we were twins. The obvious insinuation was that I simply wasn't cool enough to have a sister like Bex.

I didn't mind. It was true. I was ok with it being true. Besides, I knew her secret. I knew about the day of the pillow fort.

I would like to go on record saying that no one made a pillow fort like Bex Waller. The secret, she told me once, was that it's not just about the pillows. Only an amateur doesn't use every part of the room. Chairs, sheets, blankets, soft toys. And don't forget to fill it with entertainment. Books, games and preferably a TV. Dad didn't really like us swiping the telly in the middle of a football match, but he was impressed that Bex knew how to set it up in our room.

A couple of years after our mum left, I found my sister had made a particularly marvellous fort. 'Bex?' I called, hoping that we were about to play princess in a castle. She was the perfect princess and I was the most capable man-servant in the history of imagination. She didn't answer. I burrowed through the blanketed tunnel to get to her. 'Bex?' She was crying. 'What's wrong?'

'I've got to keep trying. I've got to! I don't want to but I've got to.'

'What do you mean?' I asked, taking her grubby little hand in my sticky one.

'How many times do you think I will have to play Mary before mummy loves us again?'

28.

I knew the real answer to that question. I also knew that sometimes the real answer didn't help, even a little bit. So I said, 'Probably just one more.'

'Good,' she sniffed. 'Because I really want to be the donkey!'

That was it. That was the one time I saw Bex as anything other than perfect. I treasured it. Not because she was sad. I'm not a sadist. It was just the one thing about my sister that no one else in the world knew. Even as she grew and she was the pretty twin and the smart twin and the funny twin all at once, I could never resent her for it. Because I knew. I knew, on the inside, she was just as small as me. I knew she never stopped trying when I never started. I knew we were the same. Only, she was so much better at being the same than I was.

But, the thing was, she never did get to play the donkey.

Monday – A trip to the office

The final days of Carole Brown – Sheffield, UK

The day after the aliens announced the apocalypse, I got up at the normal time, put on a smart black dress and a bit of make-up, and went to work. I wasn't sure what else to do. I reasoned I'd go in today, have a nosy along the way. See what everyone else was doing, and maybe I'd try something different tomorrow.

Unfortunately, the general populace was about as inspiring as Nicole from the quiz show the night before. Half of them were still crying their eyes out. The other half seemed to be getting drunk, doing drugs, or making out aggressively with what I assumed to be strangers. The most compelling thing I saw was an old lady go into an abandoned ice cream shop, and help herself to a cone with ten different flavours precariously balanced on it. She caught me watching and winked at me.

'Gotta live it up now, haven't we, love?'

I smiled to think that was exactly how dad would have spent the end of the world. Except he'd be giving the stolen ice creams to Bex and me.

30.

Other than that, I was a little disappointed in humanity. I was really hoping to see someone declaring their undying love to their best friend's girlfriend or something. Mind you, it's not like Sheffield High Street would have been a great setting for that. I ought to have gone somewhere picturesque like the Peak District, really. Maybe that's what I'd do tomorrow.

The office, perhaps unsurprisingly, appeared to be empty. I worked in a call centre, handling customer complaints for a home appliances company. I sat down at my desk and got my pen and paper out of my bag. Only then did it occur to me how monumentally stupid I was being. Who was going to be calling up to complain about their dishwasher at the end of the world?

It took three minutes before the phone rang.

'Hello, thank you for calling Things That Beep. You're speaking to Olivia. How can I help you today?'

'Olivia, is it?'

'Yes.'

'Good,' said the voice on the other end of the line. 'I just want to know whose name to put through to head office when you can't help me.'

'I'm sorry to hear that I won't be of help,' I said. 'Have a nice day.'

'Hang on a second! I haven't even had the chance to tell you what's wrong yet.'

'Oh, I'm very sorry about that. Would you like to tell me what's wrong?'

'My microwave doesn't beep anymore when it's done. I ought to sue you for all the cold meals I've had.'

'And when did this problem start?'

'This morning. Couldn't even have my usual ready meal for breakfast. You have terrible customer service.'

'I see. Let me see if I can get that sorted out for you. Could you please give me your name and warranty number?'

'I'm not giving you people anything! You just need to sort it out.'

I was about to tell them about company policy when it occurred to me just how little I cared about this right now. 'You're perfectly right,' I said. 'I'll just get a new one sent out to you and it'll be with you in five to seven working days.'

There was a silence as we both heard what I'd said and then we burst out laughing.

'Don't know what I was thinking,' said the angry customer. 'I'll just go nick one from the supermarket like everyone else. Thanks anyway, love.' I expected her to hang up but instead she added, 'Don't suppose you know where to find a toy boy, do you?'

32.

'Pardon?'

'A toy boy? You know like someone at least twenty years younger than me who's interested in knocking about with me for a bit. Was just thinking, with it being the end and everything, I ought to try it out.'

'Um, the internet?' I suggested.

'Christ, I haven't got time to be learning things like that. I'll ask my grandchildren to help me. Anyways, I'll be off then. No time to waste.'

I was about to ask her if she would take a survey on my performance, but there didn't seem to be much of a point. I hung up without even saying "bye" and waited patiently for my next call. Before it came, I heard crashing coming from the other side of the office.

It was my manager, Carole, throwing all the computers on the floor. 'Fifteen years in this sodding place!' she was yelling. 'Not head office material! Take that Marjorie!'

I was about to ask if she needed help when a voice to the side of me said, 'Fascinating.'

I can tell you with confidence that this man had never before worked at nor entered the offices of Things That Beep. I would have noticed him. For a start, because he was the best good-looking guy I'd ever seen in my life. He had this kind of ethereal beauty that made him look barely human. This was probably because he *wasn't* human. That was the second reason I knew he'd never been here before. I would have noticed the way he was floating about a foot off the ground.

I meant to ask "Who are you?" but instead I found myself saying, 'Did you know that you are breathtakingly beautiful?'

The alien tore his eyes away from Carole as she ripped out the computer keys and rearranged them in a series of rude words. 'Really?' He sounded like a voice actor playing the part of a seductive prince, only with a Yorkshire accent. 'I don't get that much.'

'You don't?' I asked sceptically. He had everything that the average person would normally consider attractive. A slender nose, high cheekbones, a square jaw, symmetrical features, pointy ears, eyes that changed colour as he moved his face about, long hair that seemed to glow a bit. 'Maybe people are too shy to tell you.'

'I don't think so,' replied the alien. 'I can always tell by how people react to me.'

Carole had finally noticed us. She waved at me and offered me a bottle of fizzy pop. I shook my head. She started shaking the bottle, laughing maniacally the whole time. Then she opened the lid, spraying us, the computers, and the carpets and everything else with sticky liquid.

34.

'Fascinating,' said the alien again. He seemed to be truly impressed by Carole's acts of vandalism. Secretly, deep down, I was a bit too. I wished I cared about anything enough to want to destroy it.

'I'm sorry,' I said. 'I don't want to be rude but this is the end of the Earth and you guys are planning to blow it up in a few days. So it seems a bit... what's the word? Oh, it was on the tip of my tongue. So annoying that it's gone like that.'

'Insensitive,' suggested the alien.

'That's right. It seems a bit insensitive for you to be here making fun of poor Carole like this. She's had a dreadful life, you know. This place was all she had.'

'Actually, I have a husband and three kids,' Carole piped up. She was shaking up her second bottle of pop.

'Actually, she has a husband and three kids,' I repeated. 'Wait a second, Carole. You have a husband and three kids? What are you doing here?'

Carole shrugged sullenly. 'I really hate Marjorie. Anyway, I could ask you the same question, Liv.'

'You could not ask me the same question! I have no husband and no kids and nobody really in the world. That's why I'm here.'

Carole looked down at the agitated bottle of pop in her hand. Then she handed it to me, said, 'I've made a terrible mistake,' and sprinted out of the office building.

When the lady who spent the apocalypse smashing up office equipment feels sorry for you, you know you're pathetic. Not sure what else to do, I undid the lid. Lemonade sprayed everywhere. Somehow, against the odds, I heard myself laughing. I laughed with my whole body, until my stomach hurt.

The alien was watching me. He looked, dare I say, charmed by me. I waited for him to say I was fascinating too, but he didn't. 'Your name is Liv?' he asked.

'Olivia Waller,' I told him. 'Liv to my friends.' I don't know why I said that. I was Liv to everyone. Carole certainly wasn't my friend. I didn't even know she had a family and she didn't even know I was miserable and alone.

'May I call you Liv?' asked the alien.

'You may. And what may I call you?'

I'd done that thing where I get drawn into people's speech patterns even though it sounds kind of awkward, and now it was clear that the alien thought this was the way people normally spoke because he said, 'You may call me Shine.'

'Cool name,' I said, just to have something to say.

'Thank you. I chose it myself.'

36.

I wasn't about to start unpacking that. 'So, Shine, how did you end up here? Tourism gone wrong? Are your people going to let you get off the earth before it blows, or are you stuck here at the end with the rest of us?'

He shook his head. Actually, he didn't really move but I got the idea he had shaken his head. 'They are not my people.'

'What? You're not part of the known-universe?'

'I am certainly not known by them.' This time, it was the idea of a smile. 'My people, well, we are always here at the end. We document planets in their final days.'

'And then you bugger off before you get blown to smithereens?' I asked.

'I like the word smithereens. It is such a rhythmic word for such a violent thing.'

'You didn't answer my question,' I pointed out.

'And you noticed,' Shine observed. 'How delightful! Do you really think I'm beautiful?'

I put my hands on my hips. 'I don't know where you're from, Shine. But around here it's considered a tad rude to fish for compliments. I've said it once, you can probably assume that I still think it.'

'I was just checking,' said Shine, and he seemed a little crestfallen. I reached over and patted him on the arm. As soon as I touched him, every part of me felt warm. 'You are smiling,' Shine pointed out.

'So?' I was suddenly defensive.

'It is not normal to smile after touching my skin.'

'What should I be doing?'

'Screaming like a thousand deaths have descended upon you.'

'Really?'

Shine laughed. 'Not really. But you ought to look a bit uncomfortable. How did my skin feel?'

'What did I say about fishing for compliments?'

He stopped floating and stood next to me. He was just a little taller than I was. 'Indulge me?'

I don't know if you've ever had an incredibly beautiful man staring intently into your eyes asking you to indulge him, but it was disarming, to say the least. I was quite proud of myself when I found the strength to say, 'No. I'll only indulge you if you indulge me.' It came out like I was flirting with him but believe me when I say I was not. I did not have the foggiest idea how to flirt with anyone, certainly not an alien. And definitely certainly not one who looked like Shine.

'Of course,' he said, magnanimously. 'You may ask your questions now.'

'Will you leave, before the end?'

'Why does it matter?'

He was right. Why did it matter? Then again, why was he answering a question with a question? Two could play at that game. 'Why do you think?'

38.

'Because if I am here to die with you, I am just part of a crazy death cult that likes getting themselves blown up with doomed worlds. If I am here to watch you and then leave you to die without helping you, I am cruel. You don't want me to be cruel.'

That was a great answer. It sounded so much better than anything I could have come up with. 'That. That's why. So which is it?'

'The death cult,' he said happily. 'I will be with you at the end, Liv.'

'With me specifically, or…?'

'With your people and your planet. Although…' His voice dropped a few registers and I nearly melted. 'You can be with me if you want.'

'I have better things to do?' It came out as a question, instead of aloof and cool-girl like I'd hoped it would.

'Perhaps, but you don't have anyone.'

I was angry. I knew I was angry because my voice got all tight and clipped like a receptionist at a busy doctor's office. 'How do you know that?'

'You just told Carole Brown as much.'

That I did. I sighed. 'What is it you'll be doing? Hanging around Sheffield city centre? Because I already had a good nosy at what everyone was doing and it was mostly drugs and…'

'I will not stay in Sheffield.'

'Why not?' I demanded, suddenly indignant on behalf of my city. 'What's wrong with Sheffield? Friendliest people on earth in this city.'

'It is not our way.'

'Oh, isn't it?' I was mollified a little. 'What's your way then?'

'There are seven days until the end. Each day I shall visit another human, selected randomly from the eight billion living on this planet. Today was Carole Brown of Sheffield, the United Kingdom.'

'And then what?'

'And then nothing. I will observe them. I will collect information on how your people live at the end of days. Then I will join you in death.'

I snorted. 'I can tell you right now, they won't be up to anything good.'

Shine tilted his head to one side. 'What makes you say that?'

'I know people. There'll be violence. Looting. War. Someone will probably try to take down the aliens. My next door neighbours have already started having marital problems and their teenage daughter has run off to join a circus. It's going to be hell on Earth.'

Shine nodded. 'Those kinds of things do happen at the end of worlds,' he acknowledged. 'But sometimes there's more good than bad. Your fellow humans might surprise you.'

'I doubt it.'

'Come with me and find out.'

Now, I want the record to show that I did try to say "no." It seemed wrong, somehow, to accept Shine's offer under false pretences. The pretence being that I wasn't sorely tempted to say "yes" just so that I could spend the next six days staring dreamily at him. I also knew that I shouldn't leave. I thought of "*DECISION DAY*" written in block capitals on my calendar. There was a competing impulse that won out. I really believed I was right about humanity. Everything was going to go to hell at the end.

But, more than anything in the world, I wanted to be proven wrong.

'How will we get about?' I asked. 'Do you have a flying saucer?'

'No,' he said. 'I have magic.'

'Magic?'

And he smiled. Actually smiled with his mouth and eyes like a normal person. Only, he went a bit too big and he looked a little crazy. He'd work it out eventually.

'Technology that can't be explained always feels like magic to those who do not understand it,' he said. He took my hand and I felt the warmth radiating up my arm again. I closed my eyes and when I opened them, we were in my living room.

'Ok, that was definitely magic,' I said.

He grinned, showing off the kind of white teeth that Americans always seem to have on the TV. 'I told you so.'

'Are you staying here tonight?' I asked, suddenly feeling ashamed for my tiny house and the fact that we could hear Max Smith shouting threats at the aliens through the walls.

'It's the least you can do when I'm going to show you the world.'

I laughed, hoping it was a joke. I wasn't sure what we were meant to do until tomorrow. 'Do you like quiz shows?'

'I have never experienced one,' Shine replied. 'How do they work?'

'Well, you just get really irrationally angry at the contestants over the most minor things, and feel smug when you know answers they don't.'

'Excellent,' he said.

Shine worked out the settee eventually, after we got through the awkward bit when he thought he was meant to sit on my lap. Once he did, we looked surprisingly normal together. If it wasn't for the glowing hair, or the colour-changing eyes, or the pointed ears, he could almost have been human. Just a really hot guy and a really average girl settling down to watch a really mundane show.

42.

'Well,' said a man called Neil with a shaky little laugh. '*I* was also going to say the fall of the Roman Empire, to be honest.'

Before I could explain to Shine that this, a contestant saying that another contestant had stolen their answer, was one of the minor things we got angry about, Shine shouted, 'No one cares, Neil!' I had never been more attracted to anyone in my life. He caught me staring at him and said, 'What?'

'Nothing,' I answered. Then, because he had earnt it, I reached out and touched his hand. 'It feels warm,' I said. 'Your skin.'

'As if you are about to burn to death?' Shine asked nervously.

'No, like nice warm. Like a bath or something. It feels comfortable.'

'Huh,' he said. 'Imagine that.'

Dreams and middle names

The history of Liv and Bex

You're probably not wondering how I ended up working in a call centre. This is the kind of thing people go out of their way *not* to wonder about. I'm going to tell you anyway. Just so you know how improbable it is for someone like me to be whisked away by a handsome alien at the end of the world.

I don't think there's many little kids who dream of being a customer support agent. I'm not saying they don't exist. I'm just saying the little boy who wants nothing more than to help Dorris figure out that her washing machine isn't turned on at the wall is in the minority. I think there's even less kids out there without any dreams at all.

I never had dreams.

Bex changed what she wanted to be ten times a week. Ballerina. Acrobat. Zookeeper. Astronaut. Writer. Actor. Fireman. Every dream you're meant to have in your childhood was, at one point or another, dreamt of by Rebecca Waller. Plus, for some reason, she spent six months when she was nine being absolutely certain she was going to grow up into an accountant. She made my dad buy her little suits and she went around saying things like, 'Urg, tax season again!' and 'Clients, eh? Don't you just want to throttle them?'

Bex never minded that I didn't have dreams. She was overflowing with them. She gave me the ones that didn't quite fit. I could be a hairdresser because she couldn't be doing with scissors and she was always going to need haircuts, wasn't she? Or I could be a rocket scientist, so that she had someone she could trust sending her to Mars.

The closest thing I ever had to an argument with my dad was when I said I wanted to leave school after my GCSEs. There was already talk of making education compulsory up to the end of 6th form, which did become law by 2015. He was worried I'd look unqualified compared to my peers.

'Unqualified for what, daddy?' I asked.

'Whatever you want to do,' he replied with a shrug.

'I don't want to do anything.' I wasn't angry exactly. I was never angry at my dad. Let's just call me annoyed.

Bex peered round the door. 'You want to be a sea lion trainer, Livvy,' she said. 'Remember so I can come to your shows.'

'Well, there we go then! I don't need education for that.'

'Rebecca Olivia Waller,' said my dad sternly, but with that twinkle in his eye adults got when talking to Bex. 'This is a private conversation.'

I saw Bex's tiny scowl before it disappeared. It wasn't that she minded being told off. She just never liked getting full-named. Our middle names had been my mum's idea. She'd called it her "little bit of whimsy." In this, as in everything, I was my sister's opposite. I loved it when dad called me "Olivia Rebecca" even if it meant I was in trouble. It felt like my last bit of her.

'Sorry daddy,' said Bex. She left the room, shutting the door behind her.

'You're not actually going to be a sea lion trainer are you?' my dad asked when we were alone.

'No,' I said.

Through the door Bex shouted, 'Oh, come on!'

'Well then, what's the harm in going to school for a few more years?' asked my dad, ignoring her. 'Pick up a few A levels. See how you feel about university after that.'

'What's the *point* in me spending another few years at school studying things I don't care about when I could get a job and start making money?'

'Education has value in itself,' said my dad softly. 'Your sister is going to…'

'I'm not my sister, am I?' I almost yelled, which took us both by surprise. I never raised my voice at him. That, like so many other things, was Bex's job.

The door flew open and my sister tumbled into my arms. 'You don't need to be me, Livvy,' she said, glaring daggers at my dad. 'You're much better being you.'

She was wrong, but it was the kind of wrong that made me feel all sad and happy at once.

My dad caved after that. I gave up school and went into the workforce. I wasn't inspired the way Liv was when she started looking at medicine for university, but I wasn't unhappy either. I worked in a bookshop for a few days and was made redundant. Then I worked as a waitress for a few years before I got "made redundant" again. Coincidently, it was right after I refused to serve a pint to someone who I suspected to be my boss' fifteen-year-old daughter wearing a fake moustache.

'You ought to sue them, Liv,' said Bex as she painted my nails the next day.

'I don't know for certain it was her.'

'Didn't you say you called her by her name and she said, "Yeah?... I mean no"?'

'Well, yes but that could happen to anyone couldn't it?'

Bex was done painting my nails. One of my hands was perfect. The other was a mess with blotches of pink all over my fingers. She caught me looking and said, 'Sorry, I had to paint that one with my left hand.'

'Why?'

'So I could practise for when I paint my own later.'

I laughed. '*Bex!*'

'What?' But she knew what, because she was grinning. 'Anyway, you really ought to do something, Livvy. It's not right, them treating you like that.'

'I know, but I don't want to. Doing something sounds harder than just moving on.'

I knew Bex didn't really get that. For her, hard wasn't a problem, not the way that unjust was. But she loved me and she knew that she didn't have to *get* everything. So she shrugged and said, 'What do you think possessed her to go with a fake moustache?'

'I don't know,' I admitted. 'It didn't really match her dress either.'

Two weeks later, I got a job in a call centre and the rest, as they say, is history.

Tuesday – Roommates

The final days of Henrietta Williams – Texas, USA

I knew we were in the US for a couple of reasons. The first was the house. It was the kind you see on the telly all the time. The kind that looks like it's made of cardboard with a big front garden that hasn't been mown in a while. I was expecting a dog on a chain to start barking at me any second.

The other reason was because of the signs out front. Some of them could have been from anywhere. The pride flags lined up in order from oldest to most recent, for instance. Or the Palestinian and Ukrainian flags. Or the "Human rights = equal rights" one. "Her body her choice," "Say their names" and the gun with a line through it started to tip me off. But where I really got the clue, was the presidential signs. Starting with Hubert Humphrey and going right up to Kamala Harris.

Shine was staring at the signs with awe in his eyes. 'Fascinating,' he said.

We picked our way through the signs and were about to knock at the door when it opened to reveal an old lady. She could have been anywhere from seventy to ninety. Her dressing gown was about ten sizes too big, and her slippers were shaped like birds. She wore a satin sleeping cap on her head.

'Oh god, people!' she said. 'I suppose you'd better come in then. Nah then, love,' she said, leading us into the house. She only addressed me, and when she looked at Shine, her nose wrinkled in disgust. 'Fancy a brew?'

To say I was confused by the fact that she spoke with an accent like my Aunty Barb's would have been an understatement. But I rolled with it. 'Uh, no thanks... love,' I said.

I would broach the topic with Shine later in the day, frowning. 'It was weird that she had a Yorkshire accent.'

Shine would frown back, 'Was it? Why's that?'

'Because she was from Texas.'

'That is factually correct.'

'Normally people from Texas have Texan accents.'

'Which one's that? Is it was the one where they say "y'all" a lot?'

'I think so.'

'Oh, good. She spoke the way she was meant to, then. Would have been mighty awkward if my electrostatic waves had permanently altered her voice. That can happen, you know?'

'But… She… I…' I shook my head. 'She *had a Yorkshire accent.*'

'Ah, I see You were hearing her through my "magical" interpreter. It lets you speak to anyone anywhere in the world.'

'But we were both speaking English. I don't understand.'

'I'm sorry,' said Shine. 'I thought I was speaking clearly. Maybe the interpreter isn't on a high enough setting. Does tha want me t' turn up the accent, love?'

'No, the way it was set before was fine, thanks,' I said quickly. 'So, will everyone have a Yorkshire accent then?'

'Of course!' he said brightly.

I was about to ask "why" again and then I realised the futility of it. 'Well, I suppose there's worse things an interpreter could do.'

'Yes, there is,' said Shine. 'One time, on the planet of Aaaaaaaa, a very highly respected interpreter incorrectly miscommunicated the depth of regard one politician had for another politician's mother. The ensuing war lasted for seven decades until the interpreter was forced to come clean.'

'Jesus, I bet they got in some trouble.'

'Not really. Unless you count being beheaded as some trouble.'

'I very much do!'

Shine chuckled. 'I forget how protective those of you with a single head can get over it.'

I was so baffled that I couldn't even bring myself to shout, "But *you* have a single head!"

But let's go back to the elderly Texan woman with the magical Yorkshire accent who had just listened to me refuse a cup of tea. We were now sitting in her living room, enclosed by four grey walls. For some reason, I was expecting the house to be brighter. But it was worn down, tired, drab.

'Suit yeh sen,' said the woman. 'What can I do for you chaps then?'

'The signs out front,' Shine ventured. 'I was fascinated by them. Where do they come from?'

Henrietta huffed a laugh. I got the impression that she'd smoked a twenty pack every day since she was about ten. 'I bought them of course. Or I made them. Especially some of the older ones.'

'And have you always had them all up front like that?'

Another smoker's laugh. 'Do I look like someone who can put signs like that out around here? No, I've been hoarding them.' She narrowed her eyes at the alien. 'How old do you think I am?'

Before I could tell Shine that it wasn't the kind of question he was meant to answer, he said, 'Very old.'

To my surprise, Henrietta laughed again. 'You're right, young'un. I'm eighty-six.' She waited for him to understand something, but he only stared at her, seemingly mesmerised. 'I'm black and I was born in the late thirties.' Her hand started rotating at the wrist, as she gestured for him not to make her spell it out. 'What does that tell you?'

'Absolutely nothing,' said Shine.

'He's an alien,' I added.

Henrietta put on her glasses and squinted at him. 'Yes, you are,' she confirmed. 'Nasty looking blighter too, sorry to say so.' She turned to me. 'But you're not, love. Care to fill him in?'

'She didn't have many rights growing up,' I told Shine.

Henrietta hooted a laugh. 'Many? Any at all would have been nice! But I'm not getting into that today. Why ruin a nice day going down into all of that… business? The point is, I was active in the Civil Rights movement. And then, because that wasn't enough grief for one lifetime, I was in the LGBT rights movement too. As you can imagine, I'm the "L."'

'I cannot imagine,' said Shine quietly so that he would not interrupt the flow of her speech.

'My roommate, Mary…' she continued, then shook her head. 'Sorry, you know what they say about old habits.'

'Does it have something to do with roommates?' Shine asked.

Henrietta seemed to be taking a shine to him, pardon the pun (or actually, don't, it's the end of the world, after all), because she said, 'Bless your heart, no! Old habits die hard.'

'That's what they say, is it?' I could tell that Shine asked this question to mask the fact that he didn't have a clue what was going on.

'It means that it's hard to get out of a habit once you've got into it,' I explained.

'Fascinating,' said Shine, his beautiful face lit up with delight. 'I'll have to remember that one. So what habit did you do with your roommate?'

'What habit didn't I do with my roommate?' said Henrietta wickedly and I laughed with her.

'I believe I have missed a joke.' Shine looked a little disappointed.

'It's an inuendo,' I explained. '"Roommate" is code for lesbian or gay partner. So Henrietta was insinuating…'

'I think I will need more context,' said Shine. 'Allow me some moments to absorb the cultural history.' Before anyone else had a chance to speak he gasped. 'I now understand the concepts of homophobia and racism. I would like to state, for the official documentation, that I am quite angry.'

Henrietta patted him on the hand and then flinched. 'You're a good lad.'

'Forgive me, Henrietta Williams,' Shine replied. 'I interrupted your story. Please go on. You were talking about your lesbian lover.'

'Right,' said Henrietta. 'She wasn't just my lover. She was the love of my life. We met protesting together. Full of fire, was our Mary. But she got an eye taken out at Stonewall. We weren't there, of course. We were out for a nice pub lunch in Brownsville. A police officer with a pal in the NYPD was in a bit of a mood about it. He didn't like that we were holding hands. Mary wanted to go on the telly about it. I told her no. No sense in reporting it either. They'd have just said it was one of our own. After that I got scared. We stopped protesting. We bought the signs but I never let her put them up.'

'I am sorry,' said Shine softly. He squeezed the woman's arm, careful to do so over her clothing. 'I wish you had been able to put up all your signs whenever you liked.'

Henrietta smiled warmly back. 'Me too. Anyway, it's suddenly about to all be over. So I thought, now or never. It took me bloody forever getting all them set up. I didn't realise I believed in so many things I was afraid to fight for.'

'Have you had any trouble? This is still a red state after all.' I was proud that I knew to ask the question. All my doom scrolling had finally come in handy for something.

'Couple of kids stole some of the lewder ones,' she said with a shrug. 'But I think most people are a bit preoccupied at the minute.'

'So, now you've put the signs out,' Shine continued. 'What is next?'

'Next? We all die, don't we? What are you talking about, what's next?'

'So you will stay here until the end?'

'Ah, I see. Yep, that's the plan. Sit here and wait for the big boom. No sense in going crazy is there, chuck?'

I looked about the house again. It looked so grey and sad. 'Aren't you lonely?' I asked.

'Lonely?' That seemed to be the funniest thing Henrietta had ever heard. 'I see what you're saying, love. You think I ought to be out there drinking or seeing the world or trying to fall in love again or seeing my family? Let me show you something.'

She got up and hobbled over to the door that led further into her house. She opened it and four birds flew into the room, perching on the furniture, making a racket, and exploring the room with their beaks. The largest one, an African great parrot, landed on her finger. 'What doing?' it asked.

'We have visitors, Judy,' Henrietta told the parrot. 'We don't want visitors but we've got them anyway.'

'Touch,' said Judy.

Henrietta brought the bird closer to me. 'She can name some objects,' she explained.

Judy bonked me on the head with her beak, once, twice, and then looked Shine dead in the eyes and said, 'It's a skull.'

'Good girl,' Henrietta crowed and fed her a pistachio.

'So the birds are your companions?' Shine asked, reaching out his finger to one of the smaller ones, a green parrot of some kind. The little bird bit his finger and he laughed with pure joy. The birds all copied the laughter, which was kind of eerie if you asked me. Not that anyone did.

'They're my family,' Henrietta explained. 'I had a sister. Still do, depending on how you look at it. But she saw me and Mary kissing once, a couple of years before Mary died. She told me I was a disgrace and she hasn't spoken to me since. She's tried to reach me a few times since the end was announced, but I was thinking about what them aliens said about figuring out what life means to you. To me, it's showing everyone everything I believe in and then hunkering down in my little house with my birds and showering them with love right up until the end.' She looked at me. 'I'm very happy, you see?'

'My mummies are gay!' announced Judy the parrot in a different voice to the one she'd spoken in so far.

Henrietta smiled, her eyes welling with tears. 'Mary's voice,' she explained. 'Mary thought it was the funniest thing in the world to teach her that. I was so afraid that would give us away but Mary said we didn't have to be afraid anymore. The world was changing. I'm glad she didn't live long enough to see it start changing back the wrong way.' She slapped her thighs. 'Well, I'm afraid I'll have to see you out now. You've been… company, but I don't want that, you understand?'

As Henrietta ushered us to the door I asked her, 'Are you really happy?'

She gave me a funny look. 'Happiest I've been since I lost Mary. I thought I was floundering, never leaving the house. Now I've realised it's what I want. No better feeling in the world than to realise I've been right all along.'

As we left the house, I turned back to look at all the signs. I wondered if there was anything I was too afraid to fight for, but the trouble was there was nothing I really believed in at all.

58.

Shine took my hand and I was glad for his warmth. The next thing I knew, I was in my living room again.

'Quiz show?'

I looked over at him and he was smiling like an idiot, his fingertip poised over the on button on the remote. 'Sure,' I said.

We watched the show for a while but he was quiet. 'I think I'm bad at my job,' he said eventually.

'What? Your job? You mean like the documenting people's stories before we all get blown up.'

He nodded. He started floating above the sofa and going in frantic little circles. 'I got too distracted looking at all the flags and just enjoying them. I could have been researching instead. I had to interrupt lovely Henrietta's story so that you could explain things to me. No one else has ever made a mistake like that.'

'You're alright,' I assured him. 'People love explaining things.'

'Even when it relates to parts of their life that cause trauma?'

He had a point. 'Probably not,' I said. 'But you'll get there. That was just day one.'

'It was day two actually. Day one was Carole Brown.'

'Exactly. You got Carole's story. I've worked with her three years and I had no idea that she had a family. You're great at this!' I actually had no idea if he was. But I thought if I didn't give him a pep talk, he might not yell at quiz shows with me again.

'Am I really?' He sounded small so I put my arm about him. The warmth flooded me.

'Absolutely,' I said. 'Now, I don't know if you noticed but Jane on the telly is wearing a really strange dress.'

'And do we get angry about that?'

'No, we don't, but we do need to comment on it.'

'Isn't that a bit judgemental?'

I leaned close to him and whispered, 'She'll never know.'

'So I could say something like, "Jane's dress looks like a dreksian cin after it's died and been left out in the sun for a few days," and it wouldn't matter?'

'Yes,' I said peacefully. 'You could say something exactly like that.'

60.

Our little gods

The history of Liv and Bex

At this point, you're probably just going to roll your eyes at me if I say that Bex had a million good causes she championed, and I had none. So I'll try to take things in a different direction and tell you that she was deeply religious.

My dad's parents were Christians, but they had a big falling out with the vicar at their church over who was meant to bring fairy buns to the Children of Jesus Picnic when dad was a baby. After that, they became atheists.

'That was how I knew God didn't exist,' grandad had told me when we were eleven. 'Because if He did, he'd never let a man like that be his preacher.'

The next day, he dropped dead of a heart attack. It was probably a coincidence. That was what my dad told me after I asked if grandad had been smited. But even he looked a bit nervous when the doctors said there had been no medical reason for it.

'I don't understand it,' said one of them, scratching his head. 'He was in perfect health. I've never seen a healthier heart.'

'In a man of his age?' my dad asked, through tears.

'No, in anyone,' said the doctor. 'It's a medical mystery. Do you mind if I write an article on this?'

Later that day, Bex came home from a sleepover at a friend's house to find me and my dad pouring over church brochures. 'What's going on?' she asked.

'You know how grandad died?'

Bex nodded. 'Yeah?'

'Well, it turns out it was God that did it. God didn't like what he said about the vicar so he smited him.'

Bex looked to my dad, hoping for some rationality but my dad just said, 'She's right. What about this one?' We had so many lovely places of worship in the UK, beautiful cathedrals, friendly temples, welcoming mosques. This was none of those things. The brochure displayed a concrete block of a building. The church's slogan was, "*Jesus knows what you did.*" This didn't scare me because I never did anything. But to Bex who may or may not have just shaved off her friend's dad's eyebrow while he was asleep and blamed it on her friend's little brother, it was a terrifying prospect.

'You don't need to go to church!' she said, rushing to sweep up the leaflets.

'We don't?' Dad put down his brochure uncertainly. 'But some of these look so nice. It's not all the way it looks on the telly, you know? Not all judgement and hellfire. There's lots of lovely, friendly churches out there. It could be a community for you girls. That was what it was for my parents before the incident with the fairy buns.'

Unfortunately, the suggestion fell on deaf ears. I didn't care about community and Bex got caught on the idea of judgement. Now she wasn't just thinking of the missing eyebrows but all the times she'd lied about being poorly so that she could skive off school. The way she'd told our teacher that one of us was adopted, and then waved off the teacher's question of, 'How would that even work?'

'I'll find a religion,' she said. 'You guys don't have to worry about it.'

A week later, she stood up at Sunday dinner and announced she was going to be a Quaker.

'A Quaker?' I asked, wrinkling my nose. 'Like one of those fluffy little Australian things we saw on that documentary where that man got beaten to death by a kangaroo.'

'Do I need to look at the parental controls on the TV again?' asked my dad.

'Don't be silly, daddy,' said Bex. 'It was just nature.' She turned back to me. 'Anyway, those weren't Quakers, they were quokkas.'

'Then, surely you don't mean the crisps? How are you going to be a crisp?' My voice dropped to a whisper. 'Aren't you afraid of being eaten?'

Bex giggled. 'No, Livvy. That's *Quavers*!'

'That's right,' said my dad. 'Quakers are the oat people who wear those old fashioned clothes.'

Oat people? I mouthed, horrified.

'Almost right, daddy,' Bex said. 'Those are American Quakers and I'm definitely not American, am I?'

'No,' I said, happy to finally have a right answer.

'Quakers are a bit Christian, so you can stop worrying about God,' Bex explained. 'They think there's a little bit of God in everyone and that everybody is important and special and good.'

'So, do you think it was the little bit of God in grandad that killed him from the inside?' I asked.

'Maybe,' said Bex thoughtfully. 'But that's ok if it was. I'll protect you both from your little gods.'

'I don't know if that means exactly what you think it does, girls,' said my dad.

'I'm pretty sure it does, daddy,' said Bex. 'Anyway, they think doing good things is more important than law. I bet they're exactly the kind of people that wouldn't judge a girl for being sent to the head master's office for singing while the teacher was talking and then not actually going to the head master's office because it was sunny out and grabbing the letter the school sent home and tearing it up before her dad saw it.'

'Bexy, did you do that?'

Bex looked at my dad, all innocent eyes. 'No, daddy, why would you say that?'

'Just a hunch,' said dad, but he was smiling.

Later on that night, Bex confessed to me that she hadn't been lying, because she hadn't torn up the letter. She'd put it in our dad's to-do pile. If there was one thing our dad never did it was go through his to-do pile.

Bex loved being a Quaker. She had my dad take her to meetings where everyone sat silently until someone felt compelled to speak. Bex often felt compelled to speak. My dad once confessed to me that it was embarrassingly often.

'She does take advantage of their goodwill,' he said sheepishly.

Then, a few months after Bex had become a Quaker, she stood up at Sunday dinner again and told us she was now Wiccan.

'What about the Quakers and our little gods?' I asked.

'I'm going to be Quaker still. I'll just be a Wiccan too.'

'Aren't those witches?' asked my dad, nervously.

'Yes! I didn't know I could be a witch as a religion. I'm very excited about it.' Bex saw my dad's face and added. 'Don't worry. It's good magic. We love nature too, us Wiccans.'

'But are you allowed to be a Wiccan at the same time as a Quaker. What about God…?'

'Oh, there's still gods in Wicca. A goddess and a god, so now I have three on my side. The Goddess, the God and the tiny God. Can't get much safer than that, can we?'

My dad gave up and helped her find a coven.

And that was what Bex did from then on. She collected religions. Any time she heard of one she found interesting, she joined it.

'All I'm saying is, that you probably don't need to practice Shintoism,' I heard myself saying to her when she called me from university. She was taking an elective on minor religions around the world. This was a very dangerous thing for Bex to do.

'Why not?'

'How many religions are you in now?'

'Twenty,' she said proudly.

'And what do you do if they contradict each other?'

'I pick my favourite bits from each one and follow that.'

'Isn't that wrong?' I asked.

She burst out laughing. 'Livvy, that's what *everyone* does.'

'Oh, is it?'

'Absolutely! Besides, a lot of them are the same when you look closely enough.'

'What do you mean?' I asked. 'How can they all be the same?'

'Mostly, all they're trying to say is be kind.'

'Do you need religion to tell you that? You're kind anyway, Bex.'

She was quiet for a long while. Then she said, 'It never hurts to have a reminder, does it?'

Wednesday – The most important job

The final days of Kim Sang Heon – Seoul, South Korea

Wednesday started with the garbled consonant noises of the Deputy Prime Minister. It was then followed by Luna's slurred, 'Hello earthlings! I hope you're all having a super end-of-everything-you've-ever-known!'

'Did you know Luna is one of only seven people in the whole universe to have studied the human language?' Shine asked brightly. 'She does a fantastic job, doesn't she?'

I was about to ask if he meant other than everyone on the planet when something occurred to me. 'Wait, is she talking in a way that everyone in the world can understand? Like, as in, it's understandable by speakers of all languages?'

Shine nodded enthusiastically. 'She is.'

'Ok, that is impressive. She does sound drunk, though.'

'That's probably because she is drunk,' said Shine with a wave of his hand.

'Oh?'

'Yes, she has a terrible problem, actually. It's quite sad. Especially for all her babies. She has a lot of babies. I don't want to spoil anything about the greater universe for you.' He paused, and then, as if he couldn't help himself, he said, 'It's over a thousand. Specifically, it's ten thousand eight hundred and twelve.'

I had no idea how to reply to that so I tuned back in to the announcement. 'And just to be very clear about this,' Luna was saying. 'This counts *all* spacecraft, not just human ones. If you were unlucky enough to be one of the Seventh Systems' Uncover Brand New Worlds Undercover trips, I'm afraid we will still blast you to death if you try to leave. Sorry about that! The Seventh System would like to remind you that you did sign a waiver about this exact scenario and they won't be entertaining lawsuits at this time. If you do want to try suing them, they request you wait until next week.' She did that thing I thought was a laugh again. 'In all seriousness, the Deputy Prime Minister would like to offer deep condolences for your tragic but inevitable deaths.'

'Hang on, so there *is* Earth tourism?' I asked Shine.

'Absolutely,' Shine replied. 'Only very recently. As in, these tourists are the first. Poor sods. Pioneerism is the ultimate flex in the intergalactic travel community. Did I use that right? "Ultimate flex."'

I didn't really know. I didn't speak like that.
'Yes,' I said with confidence.

'Excellent! I've been studying up on "the internet."'

'To wrap things up,' said Luna. 'We are all deeply disappointed at the US government for trying to send space ships containing nuclear weapons at us. Just because they blew up on their own, before we had to deal with them, doesn't make it ok. And we are even more disappointed in Max Smith, Representative of Earth, for not better policing space travel the way he said he was going to. Shame on you, Max Smith!'

'F-ing hell!' I heard Max say through the wall.

'Anyway,' trilled Luna. 'That's everything from us. Remember, just four days left until the deaths of everyone you love. Once again, that's four days until the end. So give your granny an extra big hug tonight from me. Cheerio!'

'I don't know why planets always think they can take down the Government of the Known-Universe,' Shine said sadly when the tannoy clicked off. 'It never works.'

'Out of interest, how often does the Government of the Known-Universe blow up planets.'

Shine shifted uncomfortably. 'Whenever it's necessary.'

'So, a lot.'

He nodded.

'And you don't think we ought to try fighting back. Even a little?'

Shine met my eyes. His were a lovely shade of silver at the minute, like two really shiny five pence pieces. 'It's not for me to decide. I'm just here to observe it all.'

'But you must have an opinion, right?'

Shine started to laugh as if he was going a bit mad. 'No, Liv, I mustn't have an opinion. That's one of the things about the job.'

'But you do have opinions. You think everything is fascinating.'

'It is,' Shine said slowly. 'But I'm allowed to think things are fascinating. I just can't pass moral judgement on the way people live or the universe operates.'

'You think homophobia and racism are bad,' I pointed out. I wished I hadn't as soon as I said it because all the colour drained from Shine's face. Normally that's just an expression but not in this case. He literally became translucent.

'You're right. I do. I *am* bad at my job! I knew it.'

I didn't know what else to do except pat him on the back and say, 'There, there. I don't think you are.'

'I am! I'm not impartial at all. I'm so partial. I'm terribly, terribly partial. What am I going to do?'

'Well, you've got a few more chances, haven't you? We'll go somewhere nice today and I'll have all the opinions for you.'

The colour began to return to his face. 'Ok. That sounds nice.'

'Where are we going, then?' I asked.

He reached out to me and I gave him my hand. 'It's a surprise,' he said and we disappeared.

I was a little disappointed when we materialised in a big, empty shopping centre. That was, until I looked at Shine and saw the delight on his face. I wasn't about to say anything, but he was definitely having an opinion about where we were now.

'Isn't this a marvel?' he asked.

'Sure,' I replied.

'There's a golf course, a spa, a casino, an arcade, a museum. Did you know they used to do cultural parades in here? Can you imagine that? Cultural parades in an airport! I wish I'd seen it.'

'Wait an airport?' I whirled about and started to see the signs. Literally. *Gate 1-20. Passport control. Transfers.*

'Impressed yet?'

72.

I turned back around and Shine was standing too close to me. Clearly no one had told him about personal space. I was about to take a step back when he floated around me in a circle. 'It's pretty cool,' I admitted. 'Who are we here to see?'

Shine indicated to a middle-aged man sitting alone in an empty restaurant. He was eating rice balls in the shape of bears. 'Kim Sang Heon.'

'I take it we're in South Korea?'

'No, Antarctica actually,' Shine deadpanned. Before I could laugh, he said, 'I made a human joke. Did you like it?'

'I loved it,' I told him. Shine's enthusiasm warmed my heart in a way it hadn't been warmed in a long time. One year two months and six days, to be precise.

Shine beamed at me, before floating off towards Kim Sang Heon. 'Hello!'

The man only bowed slightly in return.

'How are you spending the end of your life?'

At some point, I might have to teach Shine tact.

Although Sang Heon remained unsmiling, he did answer the question, 'Working.'

'Working?' I repeated. I was trying to think what jobs might be so important that you had to do them through the end of the world. 'Are you a doctor or summat?'

'Or summat, yeah,' agreed Sang Heon in the soft Yorkshire accent he probably wasn't actually speaking with. 'No, much more important than that right now. I'm a pilot.'

'A pilot! How wonderful! How did you get into that then?'

I was glad that Shine replied because I was grappling for an answer that wasn't just "How is that more important than a doctor?"

'I was in the military,' Sang Heon explained. 'It's mandatory here.' He looked about the empty airport and shook his head. ' *Was* mandatory. Twenty-one months in the Airforce. I was a stupid kid before that. I came out of it a stern and disciplined man. Then I moved into commercial flying, first domestic, then international. I'm a captain now, if that still matters.'

I sensed that Shine might be on the verge of having an opinion, so I said, 'It matters if it does to you.'

Sang Heon gave me his first smile of the conversation. It was small and tight lipped but it was all the better for having to earn it. 'I placed so much importance on that. Not for the money but for the superiority of it. I was a proud man.' He shook his head. 'A proud man is a bad captain. A good captain listens to his inferiors as if they were his equal.'

'Did you mean subordinates?' I felt bad asking but I also really thought I ought to.

Sang Heon cursed. 'See what I mean? I am hopelessly elitist.'

'You're still learning,' said Shine gently. 'That's quite normal, actually, to be learning right up until the end.'

Sang Heon looked at Shine properly for the first time. He did a double take and then bowed to him, far more deeply than he had when we first met. 'I surrender to your expertise, sir.'

I had no clue what was going on but I could tell Shine loved being called "sir" by the way he started preening and doing little somersaults.

'So, why are you still working?' I asked, wanting to keep us on track. 'Why not spend your last days having fun?'

Sang Heon nodded. 'That was what I thought too. It is what many of my colleagues did, hanging up their wings to spend these precious last days with family and friends. We were in the air when the announcement came. I don't have anyone, so I thought I would go home and eat well and enjoy my final days with a few good books. I told the First Officer this, and he said, "That's a shame." He didn't elaborate and I didn't think to ask more at the time. I was mildly distracted by the fact the world was ending and I had a plane full of screaming people to

contend with. The lady in seat 23A was causing a ruckus. She wanted us to try and fly out to space in our Airbus A320. I knew this because she got them all shouting it. "Fly to space! Bugger up the aliens!"'
He shook his head. 'The daft apaths.'

I didn't want to admit that I didn't know that planes didn't go to space, so I just said, 'How silly of them.' And he nodded approvingly.

'Anyway, I thought about it a lot after, what my FO said. I wondered what he meant.'

'What did he mean?' I asked, intrigued.

'I do not know. It was the only time I'd ever flown with him. I had no way to contact him. There are so few people still working. No one to connect us. But, I found my own meaning for it. There are so many people with places they would like to be, now at the end of times. Perhaps they have never travelled and want to see the pyramids. Perhaps they have family in Kenya and they want to say goodbye. I realised I could help those people. That is why I work.'

Now I understood why he had said being a pilot was more important than a doctor. He was right. I stared at him, open-mouthed.

'But surely there are more people who would like to fly than pilots to fly them,' said Shine. 'How do you choose?'

Sang Heon bowed his head. 'That part is easy, sir. We take those who have had the least opportunity to travel before. We take the poorest.'

'But how do you know who's poorest?' I asked. 'Wouldn't they just lie to get on the plane?'

'We have help, tax collectors, hackers, government officials. You would be surprised how many politicians are decent people when there's nowt to campaign for.'

'If it's more than zero, I *would* be surprised,' I agreed, and Sang Heon flashed me a full grin.

'We do our best to check, but sometimes we can't find the necessary data in time. Sometimes, it just comes down to trust.'

'But how can you?' I asked. 'Wouldn't anyone lie to see their family at the end of the world? How can you believe them?'

Sang Heon regarded me thoughtfully. 'You think people are generally selfish,' he said.

'Maybe.' I wanted to say "yes" but I was thinking of Bex. All the times she loved me more than she loved herself.

'That's what I thought too,' said the pilot.

'But you don't anymore?'

He shook his head. 'I lived my life selfishly but, in the end, it turned out I am capable of doing good. I believe, now, that people are more good than bad.'

'Isn't that naïve?' The question slipped out before I had a chance to think about what I was saying.

'Perhaps, but I'd rather be naïve than cynical. If people won't do right here at the end, I would rather not know. What I'm doing now, the looks on people's faces. I have never felt so…'

'Happy,' Shine suggested. He was floating cross-legged about a foot off the ground, and leaning close to the pilot, hanging on his every word.

Sang Heon considered it and settled for, 'Hopeful.'

Shine nodded sagely. 'Of course,' he said.

78.

The ocean

The history of Liv and Bex

Do you know what people who are abandoned by their mothers are famous for doing? Not trusting anyone with a ten foot barge pole. I stuck to this rule, Bex didn't.

When she came home from uni for Christmas, she looked taller and more tanned. An impressive feat since she'd only been up in Newcastle. That first evening she talked animatedly about her life in a brand new accent.

'And wor Katie is a reet bonnie lass. She cannet gan doon toon without some laddie or other trying to neck her.'

When she went to the loo, I turned to my dad. Before I could speak, he shrugged and said, 'Not the foggiest.'

Later that evening, as I was going to bed, I walked past Bex's room and heard her through the door.

'Whey aye. Whey *aye*. *Whey* aye. Whey aye, man.'

'Bex?'

'Hello!' she said, and then, 'I mean, areet?'

I opened the door. 'Bexy?'

'The accent's fake,' she blurted out.

'No? Is it really?'

'Don't tell daddy.'

'We really ought to. He doesn't have a clue what you're saying.'

She grinned at me mischievously and I realised that was the point.

'Are you really having a good time, Bex? Up in Newcastle.'

'Oh, I love it! No one parties like a Geordie and everyone's so pretty and happy. I have so many new friends.' And she went on to tell me about them all, this time using words I understood.

Katie spoke like the queen and she looked like a princess. She was a sweetheart too. She had been the most worried of everyone when Bex disappeared on that fateful night out. She'd been on the verge of calling the police when Bex turned up again three hours later, sitting at the foot of the Grey's Monument, wearing a hat with bear ears.

Safia was the bold one. She didn't drink but she was braver sober than the rest of them were drunk. She had been responsible for starting the chorus of Bohemian Rhapsody that had got them banned from their favourite pub.

'You got banned for singing?'

'I don't think you understand just how out of key we were, Livvy.'

Lucy was the funniest person in the world. I should hear her bit about her friend, Tom, trying to take a twelve inch machete to a gig. The way she imitated his voice as he was being carted away behind a dark curtain to have the police called on him. All shy and awkward, 'Oh, don't kick me out. I'll be *so* embarrassed if I get kicked out in front of my friends.' No, that wasn't quite right. You had to be there to hear Lucy do it.

'Just out of interest, why did he try to take a twelve inch machete to a gig?' I asked.

Bex shrugged. 'How should I know?'

Anyway, the point was that Bex could never catch her breath for giggling whenever Lucy was around. I pictured the two of them together, folded over, crying with laughter, and smiled.

Bex went on and on like this. There were so many people in her life now. I could have thought my way round to being jealous, but I wasn't. I loved seeing her like that, all bright and shiny.

'How's your course going?' I asked when she finally took a breath.

She waved a dismissive hand through the air. 'It's all heart this and brain that.' Then her eyes shone. 'Oh, but, Livvy, there's a boy in my infectious disease class.'

'There's a boy?'

'There's a *boy*,' she confirmed. The way she said it, with her eyes all big and googly, I could tell she was already a goner.

The boy's name was John. This is, coincidently, also the first name of Willoughby in Sense and Sensibility. He was handsome, intelligent, charming, funny. She'd had boyfriends before. Ten of them, starting with the time she marched up to Luke Taylor when she was eleven and told him she liked the shape of his knees. This was different. John was different. He scared her in the best possible way. By the time she came home for Christmas, she had progressed no further than peering at him from round the side of her textbook.

She hoped simultaneously that he would and wouldn't notice her. And was disappointed that he didn't. I found that hard to believe. She was beautiful, smart and wonderful. Bex said there were a lot of beautiful, smart and wonderful girls in her class. Didn't I remember Katie? Maybe I was biased but I couldn't imagine anyone drawing more attention than my sister. She was the sun to me.

Then they were put together for a group project, a case study on malaria. There were three of them. Bex, John and a kid called Aaron who had showed up to lectures a grand total of three times since the start of term.

82.

Aaron had always performed well in school because he had been motivated by the fear of his parents taking away his game consoles. Once he moved away from home, he realised there was nothing his parents could do to him. He was on track to fail his first year, until he ran away in the second term to join a circus. He became a lion trainer and met a fateful end. More specifically, he ended up in prison because he didn't pay his taxes.

Bex despised Aaron. 'What kind of a person wants to keep the king of the jungle in a tiny cage?' she asked in disgust. The use of wild animals in circus acts was outlawed in the UK in 2020, but Shine told me that the circus Aaron worked for kept their lions illegally right up until the end. Then, on Monday 3rd March 2025, in the chaos that followed the announcement of the end of the world, the lions got free and mauled most of their captors to death. I didn't want to say good riddance, so I just thought it really loudly.

The other reason Bex hated Aaron was that he left her waiting alone in a café when he was meant to be meeting up to work on their group project. She'd half expected it. That didn't mean she wasn't allowed to be angry about it. Getting angry at things was one of Bex's hobbies. And, even more than Aaron, she was furious with John.

John finally showed up two hours later. He had ignored her texts and calls and she had done much of the project herself. She was ready for him. She looked like a super villain, her eyes narrowed, sipping her coffee vindictively.

'Hello,' he said. 'Rebecca, right? Sorry I'm late, I...' He trailed away. 'Where did you get that cat from?'

Bex ran her hand through the black fur menacingly. 'That's none of your business.'

He pulled a chair opposite her and gave her his most engaging smile. 'I really am sorry, Rebecca.'

'Go on then.'

'Sorry?'

'Why are you late, Joe?' Bex thought using the wrong name was a stroke of genius.

It certainly seemed to throw him. 'Um, it's John.'

'Why?'

'Why is my name John? It was my grandad's name. He died the same week I was born and my mum thought maybe he'd been reincarnated as me.'

For a second, Bex was thrown off track. 'Really? What religion does she follow? Actually, that's not the point. Why are you late? And, to be clear, the explanation better cover why you haven't answered my texts or calls or I'll set the cat on you.' The cat in her lap rolled onto its back and started purring.

'I...' John began. 'I...'

'That's what I thought.' She pushed her chair away from the table aggressively.

'Wait, please,' said John.

Bex didn't want to wait. She wanted to get up and storm out, but there's something quite undignified about trying to unhook a cat's claws from your thighs as it yowls to stay put. So she said, 'What?' as if it had always been her intention to hear him out.

'I fainted giving blood. I didn't have my phone with me and they didn't want me to leave until they were sure I was alright.'

Forgiveness began to creep in. 'Why wouldn't you just say that?'

'Because it's kind of embarrassing and you are... I mean, Christ, you're beautiful.'

Bex did her best to keep glowering at him but her heart had gone into overdrive. In the end, she said, 'Fine. You can stay and finish the project with me. And you can call me Bex.'

When they were nearly done studying for the day, John leaned across the table and stared up at her with a smile on his face. He looked so handsome she could scream. 'Do you want to come to a party with me tonight?'

'Ok,' said Bex, both because she never turned down the chance to go to a party and because she couldn't have said "no" to John if she wanted to. 'But set your expectations low.'

John set his expectations high and was rewarded accordingly. Bex put a lot of effort into putting together an outfit that made her look like she hadn't tried, whilst also making her look incredibly hot. When he saw her he wolf whistled and said, 'Damn!' She scowled back while butterflies played in her stomach.

The next morning, she called me. 'He kissed me!' I didn't have to ask who.

Bex and John were together for four years. I'm ashamed to say I liked him. He made me laugh. He took the time to talk to dad about the boat he was completely and absolutely going to own one day. He went with Bex to a number of her religious meetings and ceremonies and rarely complained about it.

I missed all the red flags. Wilfully, I think. Like the way he cut her off when she started to rant excitedly about something. I loved Bex's enthusiasm for the world. Her brain was a sponge. She knew about everything from nuclear fission to earthworms. I could listen to her talk all day.

But, with John around, she'd get no further than, 'Did you know that one time a plane had it's whole top ripped off and only one person died because...'

before he'd ruffle her hair and say, 'My little know-it-all.'

At the time, I thought he was being affectionate. In hindsight, it made me angry. Because whenever he did that, Bex immediately stopped talking. After they broke up, she told me that, when they were alone, the way he said "know-it-all" wasn't so affectionate anymore. He told her she made everyone else feel stupid. A guy didn't want his girlfriend to be smarter than him. It was just basic biology. When she confessed this, in a small voice, my dad scoffed and said, 'If he thinks sexism is "basic biology," I fear for the future of the NHS.' Which seemed to make Bex feel a little bit better.

There was also the way John looked at me sometimes. Like he was trying to picture me naked. It made my skin crawl. It made me want to cover myself up with a tent.

'It's unrealistic to think he'd only have eyes for me,' Bex said once, when we saw him staring at a pretty girl at the park.

I accepted the explanation gladly. I wanted so badly to believe in her fairytale. I didn't need my own happy ever after as long as Bex could have hers. So what if Prince Charming had wandering eyes? I didn't know how wrong she'd been until she finally met someone good, years later. Because, while her someone good did occasionally find other women attractive, he didn't ogle them the way John did. And it was quite obvious that, for him, no one came close to comparing to Bex. But I'm getting ahead of myself. We have to deal with John first.

Bex showed up at our house on a Tuesday morning. I was still rubbing sleep from my eyes after working late the evening before. 'No class today?' I asked. She didn't reply. 'Bex?'

'It's over between me and John.'

'What? Why?'

'You know my friend Katie? He's been messaging her. Sometimes he seemed a little too friendly, and she wasn't totally comfortable with it, but she thought she was probably reading too much into things. She's so trusting, is Katie.'

I rubbed her back, thinking I could say the same for her.

'Anyway, yesterday he sent her this.'

She showed me her phone. A screenshot of a conversation between Katie and John.

John: *Katie, I know I shouldn't say this but I like everything about you. I think you're the most beautiful girl I've ever seen. I don't want to do this to Bex but I can't help the way I feel. I think you feel the same. Please tell me you feel the same and we'll figure it all out together.*
Katie: *Go screw yourself, John.*

'I feel like such an idiot,' she cried.

'You're not an idiot! He's an idiot.'

'He's not wrong. Katie is beautiful.'

'So are you. And she's your *friend*! What kind of selfish, stupid guy…?'

'I love him still,' she interrupted me before I could finish my sentence.

I didn't know what to say after that, so I just held her and cried with her, until she couldn't take it anymore and shut herself in her room, away from the world.

Later that evening, while I was brushing my teeth, I heard my dad knock on her door. 'Bex,' he said softly.

'Leave me alone!'

But my dad knew the difference between a real "leave me alone" and one that actually meant "I want you to come into my room and give me a hug but I'm too afraid to be vulnerable."

'I don't think you'll thank me for what I'm about to say,' he said. 'It's going to hurt. I couldn't have heard this about your mum when she left, but I need you to hear this. John was a surface person.'

'A surface person?' I heard Bex ask.

'Everything that's good about him is only *this* deep.' I imagined him holding a thumb and finger an inch apart. 'And you, Bex, you're the ocean.'

Bex dissolved into tears again. I imagined my dad holding her and I felt a bit better. After a while, she said, 'Do you still believe in love?'

I froze. We never asked dad about his love life. It was an unspoken thing between us. There hadn't been anyone for him since mum.

'Of course I do,' he said.

'Me too,' Bex whispered. And I've never felt further from understanding either of them. 'You know, I'm really happy Katie told me. It means I can trust her, doesn't it?'

'Yes,' said my dad. 'Katie's a lovely girl.'

She really was. Years later, she would be a bridesmaid at Bex's wedding. She would look so incredibly beautiful in her olive green dress that a distant relation of the groom would make a comment about how Bex ought to have put her in something unflattering. Bex, with her new husband's arm about her waist, would say, 'Thanks for the tip, Sarah. I'll remember that for the next one.' And they'd laugh and laugh and laugh. So confident there would never be a next one. And there never was.

'I think you might be right about John,' Bex said quietly. 'And I still love him. What does that say about me?'

'Only good things,' my dad assured her.

Now, I wouldn't say I was actively eavesdropping on their conversation this whole time. I was just taking my dental hygiene very seriously. If it just so happened that I could hear every word they said from the bathroom, then what could I do about that? But there's only so many times a girl can brush her bottom, back-right molar. I was about to sneak to my bedroom, when I heard Bex say, 'Livvy's the ocean too, isn't she, daddy?'

'Yes, she is.'

'I wish she knew that.'

My dad sighed. 'Me too,' he said. 'Me too.'

Thursday – The Yorkshire pudding of fears

The final days of Julian Ngaio – New Plymouth, New Zealand

We were late. I didn't know it was possible to be late to meet someone who wasn't expecting you, but Shine assured me that it was. We'd stayed up until an ungodly hour watching quiz shows and overslept this morning. I said "sorry" because it was what I was most comfortable doing whenever anything went wrong.

'But *I* was the one who wanted one more episode,' Shine pointed out as he rushed about frantically. 'And it wasn't just one more episode. Why didn't I work out that it was never going to be just one more episode?'

I grappled for a way to make it my fault. 'You wouldn't even know about quiz shows if I hadn't introduced you to them.'

Shine stopped moving to stare at me earnestly. 'Oh, but I'm glad you did, Liv. I have learnt so much about the Earth and humanity. Who knew it would be so infuriating to watch perfectly nice people make small and innocent mistakes?' He looked at the clock on the wall. 'Oh dear, look at the time. What am I going to wear?'

We left five minutes later, after I had gently pointed out that Shine only seemed to own one outfit, a long hooded cloak type thing. And after he turned into a literal puddle of embarrassment over the blunder. And after he'd had to grow himself back up from scratch.

'The bones are always the hardest bit,' he grumbled.

When we arrived at our destination, three things happened at once. The first was that I heard raucous and cathartically pleasing screaming. The second was an elbow colliding with my side. The third, was that Shine tripled in size, his eyes turned red and his teeth became fangs.

'*DO HER NO HARM*,' he said in a voice that sounded like it came from the depths of hell.

'No one's going to hurt your girlfriend, love,' said a man with long hair and tattoos. 'But it's not on to show up out of nowhere in the middle of a mosh pit. Now you've ruined the atmosphere.'

I blushed and said, 'I'm not his girlfriend,' at the same time as Shine, with the biggest smile on his face, said, 'Did you hear that Liv? He thinks I could be your boyfriend!' He'd mostly returned to his normal, pretty-boy form by this point, but he still had the pointy teeth. Would you judge me if I said they were kind of hot? I blame the popularity of YA paranormal romance books in my formative years.

'By the way what's a mosh pit?' Shine asked. The man stared at him opened-mouthed. 'You're very right, sorry. I'll look it up myself.'

'Yeah, you do that,' said the man, turning back to the stage.

I took in my surroundings. We were noticeably at a gig. It was an outdoor venue, lined by trees. On stage was a screamo band, a perfect blend of loathing oneself or one's father and having the lung capacity of a blue whale and a throat of steel to express said hatred. Bex loved this kind of music. When I told her I didn't get it, she said, 'Just imagine they're singing about mum.' That didn't work for me. I could never bring myself to hate our mother the way Bex could.

'Does your auto-translator work on signs too?' I asked Shine.

'Yes, why?'

'No reason,' I said.

One of the screens next to the stage read, "*The Gig at' End o' t' World*" and the other read, "*All genres. Does tha not like our music? Gi' it a few minutes.*"

Even now that the mosh pit had dissipated, the crowd was still more densely packed than I normally would have been able to tolerate. But, right now, I was in awe of it. There was something so beautiful about all these people, thousands and thousands of them, enjoying the same thing at the same time. Jumping and head banging and dancing and waving their arms in the air. I felt like I was part of something.

'Ah, good, there's another one,' said the man. 'Have a good one, chaps.' And he pushed his way through the crowd to join a mosh pit that was forming in front of a five foot nothing girl with pink hair. She threw her hands up in the air and said, 'Every bloody time!'

'I have now concluded my research on mosh pits,' declared Shine. 'Fascinating things. Despite having consumed three hundred academic papers and several thousand social media posts, I really have no idea why humans make them. And do not get me started on the "wall of death." It's all completely baffling.' He watched the girl with pink hair get knocked down. A giant of a man picked her up with one hand and looked at her with concern. 'Perhaps we should join that one as research.'

'Bex used to start them,' I said, mostly to distract him.

'Your sister? Did she say why?'

'She said there was something nice about them. No one is actually trying to hurt each other. They're all just trying to process all their big feelings together. She said it was like having new friends for a few minutes.'

'Fascinating,' said Shine. Then his eyes went soft. 'Liv?'

'Yes.'

'Did you want to tell me about your sister?'

I did. I really did. From the sympathetic look he was giving me, I wondered if he already knew. I couldn't find the words. So I said, 'Who are we here for?'

'The band? I don't know, but I liked the part where the lead singer connected his loneliness to the fact his father was a worm. What an excellent piece of introspection. I can only imagine how difficult it must have been to grow up with an invertebrate as a parent, especially one lacking in the power of speech. I am what is known as a hyper-vertebrate, although I am able to make all my bones disappear for comedic effect.'

'I don't think he meant...' I cut myself off. 'Wait, did you turn into a puddle earlier as a joke?'

Shine nodded. 'I was a little hurt when you didn't laugh,' he admitted. He looked it too, and I had to fight the urge to give him a hug.

'I wasn't asking about the band anyway. I meant whose last days are we experiencing.'

'Oh,' said Shine. 'Julian Ngaio of New Plymouth, New Zealand.'

'And which one is he?'

Shine shifted uncomfortably. 'I don't know.'

'What?'

'I told you we were late.'

'And that means you don't know?'

'I know he's somewhere in this crowd,' Shine mumbled.

I said nothing. The crowd was at least ten thousand people.

'I'll recognise him when I see him.'

'Just out of interest… I'm not trying to say anything here but what happens if you don't find him?'

'Oh no, Liv! Don't you believe in me?' He looked so truly horrified that I smiled.

'You're adorable.' It slipped out before I could think what I was saying.

'And beautiful too?' Shine asked, changing between dismay and delight with the flip of a switch.

Before I had the chance to tell him off for compliment fishing, a slim man moved between us. While other concert goers used their elbows to get wherever they wanted to go, this man picked his way through carefully, saying, 'Sorry, could I just squeeze past you. Sorry. I, um, just need to… Thanks.'

'That's him!' said Shine brightly.

'Shouldn't you grab him?'

'No need.'

'But he's getting away!' I pointed out. 'Don't you need to talk to him?'

'I don't think he's going far,' said Shine.

He was right. Julian Ngaio made his way, slowly and politely, into the mosh pit. Then he began ramming people with his entire body.

'Huh!' I said, and caught Shine watching me grinning. 'Shouldn't you be observing him instead of me?'

'I was,' Shine lied. His eyes darted quickly back to the small figure throwing himself at much larger men in the mosh pit. 'His tattoos are beautiful, aren't they? I wonder what they mean.'

'I think he's Maori,' I said. Shine was looking at me again, this time his expression blank. 'The indigenous people of New Zealand.'

'Indigenous people?'

'Yes, you can… Actually, whatever you do, don't look it up. You'll only learn about colonialism, and then you'll definitely have an opinion.'

'Ok,' said Shine. 'I won't.' Less than thirty seconds passed. Then he said, 'Liv, I accidentally looked up colonialism and you were right. I do have an opinion.'

I was silent as I tried to find a creative way to say "I told you so."

'My opinion is that it was a very bad thing,' Shine added, just in case it wasn't clear.

The band finished their last song. The cheers and woops were deafening. Over in what had been the mosh pit, Julian Ngaio clapped awkwardly. 'Thank you New Plymouth! You have been amazing! We will remember this gig for the rest of our lives!' The field filled with the sound of over ten thousand people collectively laughing at their own impending doom. 'We've been Bleeding from the Eyes. Now join me in welcoming the next act to the stage. The incredibly talented Little Mimi!'

'They really weren't kidding about the genre changes, were they?' I asked as a country singer dressed like Little Bo Peep took to the stage and began to sing a ballad about killing possums.

Shine wasn't listening to me. He was all business, cutting through the crowd to make his way to Julian Ngaio who was now making an awkward, but incredibly swift, beeline towards the back of the field. I struggled to keep up. I felt Shine pulling me in front of him. Together, we glided ethereally through the crowd. It was kind of weird, actually. I definitely lost some of my corporeal being in the process. Shine swept Julian up too.

'Oh, thank you,' said Julian. 'Terribly kind. Just this music isn't my cup of tea. I had a pet possum growing up. Don't tell the authorities. Mindscha, I suppose they wouldn't care now. Maybe I could get another one.' Then he looked up at Shine and gulped. 'Are you…?'

'He's an alien,' I confirmed. 'But not the same kind who are going to blow us all up.'

Julian nodded. He still looked uncertain. 'Right, I see.'

Shine set us both down on the little hill at the back of the field. 'What a lovely day!' he declared. Julian and I exchanged a look. I think he must have been talking about the music because it was raining in that way that gets you wet.

'Um, I guess,' said Julian.

Shine nodded approvingly. 'So, Julian, Liv was just telling me about colonialism. I hope you're doing ok.'

'Uh, I think I'm fine, thanks. I mean, we're all going to die anyway, so…' He looked at me. 'I guess you're Liv,?'

I nodded. 'I didn't tell him anything. He did his own research. He does a lot of that.'

'Right…' Julian looked uncertainly between the two of us and then he brightened. 'You know, you're really pretty. What are you doing tomorrow?' he asked me.

'Oh, I don't know. We'll be somewhere else then, I think. Why?'

'What about right now, then? Want to go steal a nice dinner with me or something?'

I gave the question some thought. Julian was good looking in his own way, and he was interesting too. I was curious how this awkwardly polite man was the same one who put his whole weight into elbowing people in the ribs in a mosh pit. I opened my mouth to answer when Shine asked, 'Is this how humans begin romantic relationships?'

Julian blushed. 'Kind of.'

'Fascinating. But I'm afraid we won't be here for long.' He put his arm about my shoulders rather protectively. I wondered if he even knew he was doing it.

Julian held up his hands. 'Sorry, I didn't know.'

Shine blinked. 'Didn't know what?'

'You're acting like my boyfriend again,' I explained.

Shine smiled, his mouth inhumanly wide. 'Excellent!'

I was going to tell him that it was decidedly not excellent, but there was something so endearing about Shine's joy. 'Sorry,' I said to Julian. 'I'm not really doing the hooking up at the end of the world thing. I'm doing the exploring the world with an alien who has no concept of boundaries thing instead.'

Julian laughed. I couldn't help but think how often Bex made people laugh like this, and how rarely I did.

'Sing it with me,' called Little Mimi up on the stage.

'Death to possums!' The crowd sang, off-key in a thousand different ways. 'Death to possums! Kill them all!'

Julian covered his ears. It looked like the music was physically hurting him. Shine reached out and touched him on the head. Julian tentatively moved a hand and then blinked up at the alien. 'What did you do?'

'I made it so you can only hear us for now. I hope you don't mind.'

'Not at all,' said Julian. 'It's actually exactly what I needed. I keep thinking of little Reggie and his tiny toes.'

'Reggie was the possum?' Shine asked.

Julian nodded. 'Yes, so you did me a favour. Now I'm *proper* sorry for hitting on your girlfriend.' He gave me the kind of look I'd seen so many people give Bex before. 'But can you blame me?'

'I certainly do not blame you,' Shine said, before I could point out again that I wasn't his girlfriend. 'It's my job not to blame anyone for anything. I am curious, though. What made you "ask her out"?'

'Other than the fact she's gorgeous?'

'Well, yes, other than that.'

I normally wasn't a big fan of men talking about me as if I wasn't there, but it didn't feel like they were being sleezy. It was as if they were referencing something so obvious it hardly needed saying. Olivia Waller is gorgeous and the sky is blue. To be honest, I was quite flattered. I let it lie.

'It's the same reason I'm here, actually,' said Julian. 'I have three brothers. They're all big guys. Two of them play rugby professionally and the third is a white water rafting guide. My mum always said that I was her sensitive little soul. She'd joke that I was the one who'd live long enough to look after her in her old age.' He paused. I knew that look in his eyes. I reached out to squeeze his hand.

'She didn't live to old age?' Shine asked gently.

'She died a year ago. Cancer.' He shrugged but I could see the weight of the world was on his shoulders. 'I wrote a list then. All the things I'm scared of.' He grimaced. 'It's a long list. A really long list.'

'And hitting on Liv is on there?'

Julian smiled shyly. 'Number fifteen – ask out a beautiful girl. I've had a few girlfriends but I never had the courage to just see someone I thought was a hottie and go for it.'

'So you have been going through this very long list for a year and Liv was the first hottie you came across?'

Julian met my eye and we both burst out laughing.

'Not exactly,' Julian choked through fits of laughter. 'I actually only started on the list this week. I've been putting it off. I had a lot of time, until I didn't. So I started the morning by saying "no" to a friend asking for a favour. I felt quite bad about that one. He wanted me to watch his dog for the day so he could take his grandma to her favourite place for the last time. But it *was* on the list. I never say "no" to anyone normally. Then I came here to face my fear of crowds and violence. And, luckily enough, I was also able to get rejected by a girl who is way out of my league.'

'Is there an order to it? Are you afraid of all these things equally? Crowds and women and saying "no."'

'Uh.' Julian chuckled nervously. 'Not exactly. Asking your friend out was definitely the most terrifying thing I've ever done. Especially since my fear turned out to be justified.'

'Sorry about that,' I said, wincing. 'I mean, I do think you're attractive. I just… don't really have time for it.'

Julian beamed at me.

'Oh yes,' said Shine. 'All humans are attractive in their own way.' He was entirely oblivious to the disappointed look on Julian's face. 'So what are you most afraid of? Are you saving it for last like Liv does with Yorkshire puddings?'

I wondered if Yorkshire puddings got translated into some New Zealand delicacy for him. What did New Zealanders like? I made a mental note to ask Shine later and never did. It's funny the things you forget when everything and everyone you've ever known is about to be blown to pieces, isn't it?

'Yes, actually, I am,' said Julian.

'And what are you most afraid of? What's the plan for the end?'

Julian looked up to the sky. Then he said, 'Mountains.'

I had questions. So many questions. Specifically mountains? Or was it heights? Or volcanoes? Was it the climbing them? Or just looking at them?

Shine only had one, 'So that's what you'll do last? Climb a mountain?'

Julian looked exceedingly nervous, but he nodded. 'That's the plan.'

Again? Again!

The history of Liv and Bex

Some people when they go through a nasty break up dye their hair a different colour. Some take comfort in friends. Others go on the rebound, or throw themselves into their work or exciting new projects. Start taking risks in other parts of their lives. That's what Bex did after John.

All of it.

The hair came first. Bex chose to keep her blonde, but added a rainbow underlayer. She loved it. It was just as bright as her. It had the double benefit of delighting children and scaring homophobes away. The mere sight of a rainbow could reduce the most powerful bigot to a quivering wreck. They'd barely force out, 'I don't have a problem with lesbians but…' before the brilliance of my sister's hair forced them into a swift retreat. At least that was what Bex said. Her friend, Saf, told me it had something more to do with all the scathing put downs Bex used when she realised why they were giving her dirty looks.

A couple of months after the break up, Bex decided it was time to get back out there. No sense breaking her heart over John forever. She was a little worried she might have lost her mojo, but I don't think that was humanly possible for Bex. She was still the same girl who always played Mary in the nativity. Her first date after John was with a lovely guy called Fred. She had a nice time. She didn't think it'd go anywhere. But he was keen so she decided to give it another couple of dates.

Two months later, she called me in a panic. 'Liv, he just told me he loves me. What should I do?'

'I take it you don't love him back?'

'Well, he's very sweet and he did help me that time I got trapped in my room because there was a spider living in the doorway. I might have starved to death if he hadn't valiantly thrown it out the window.'

'Bex?' I said, trying not to laugh.

'Still no spark,' she said sadly. 'None of that making my insides all gooey thing that John did.'

I didn't say anything.

'I know. I need to break up with him. I'll do it tomorrow.'

Reader, she did not do it tomorrow.

In fact, she never did it at all. Another month down the line, Fred left her. He didn't believe in organised religion, and she did. Specifically, she believed in organised religions, plural. He asked if she'd be willing to convert to atheism.

'Sorry, Fred,' she said. 'You're a sweetheart but atheism is the one religion that I can't add to my collection. I have no idea how I'd get all my gods to agree to that.'

So they parted ways amicably. It took half a day for Bex to call me, crying. 'I think maybe I did love him.'

She didn't. Bex had just always had a hard time letting go. I comforted her as if her heartbreak was real.

After Fred, Bex couldn't even stomach going on dates. She focused on other things instead, her career, her friends, us. I didn't want to say, but it seemed like a distraction. I didn't think she was over John. I inferred this when she said, 'I don't think I'm over John.'

'Oh?' I said as casually as possible.

'I saw him with his new girlfriend and I wanted to cry. And, after that, I did cry.'

'I'm sorry Bexy. She's got nothing on you.'

Bex's eyes widened. 'I should hope not! I've done my best to keep on the good side of the law. Someone blackmailing me is the last thing I need.'

'No, I meant she's not as good as you.'

'Oh. How do you know?'

'Because no one is as good as you.'

Bex gave me a tight hug. 'Thanks, Livvy. But let's not do that. I don't want any more beef with a girl who's probably perfectly lovely.'

'You're right. It's not her fault that John… Wait a minute. Did you say "*any more* beef"?'

Bee smiled sheepishly. 'She thinks I'm a bit weird.'

'Why would she think that?' I was outraged.

'She met me on a bad day.'

My nostrils flared. 'Well, that's no reason to…'

'It was the one where I was following John around everywhere standing really close to him.'

'Ah, that'll do it.'

'She wanted him to get a restraining order against me and I had to promise to restrain myself.' Bex half laughed. 'Love is really weird, isn't it?' Before I could answer, she went on, 'By the way, on a related note, you know how it's my birthday at the end of the month?'

'I'm vaguely aware.'

'Well, I booked us both to go sky diving. My treat!'

Bex must have known I wouldn't like this. I could tell by the way she tripped over her laces trying to run away from me.

I towered over her as she lay on the floor rubbing her shins. 'No.'

'You have to. It's my birthday.'

'It's my birthday too!'

'What does that have to do with anything?'

'Bex!'

'Sorry, worth a shot.' When I didn't answer she added, 'Please. I think it'll help me get over John.'

'Are you just saying that to manipulate me?'

'Maybe. Is it working?'

'I'll think about it.'

She squeezed my hand. 'Thanks, Livvy.'

Now, you might have guessed this already, but I never intended to go sky diving. I let Liv sign me up, thinking I'd back out before the day. I had a cunning plan involving my dad. He'd been peppering me with questions for days.

'How far will you jump from?'

'I don't know, daddy. I'm trying not to think about it.'

'Are you doing it round here?'

'Yeah.'

'Where abouts?'

'Not sure. Bex arranged it.'

'Is there an age limit?'

'I'm not sure, dad. Why? Do you fancy it?'

'No, not at all. Just wondering.'

I told myself two or three days before, I'd start to feel like I was coming down with something. I imagined curling up in bed, clutching my stomach and saying, "This sucks. I really wanted to go.

Maybe I can... No, alas, moving is no good! Maybe we'll just have to see if daddy can take my spot."

This idea was squashed when, four days before our birthday, my dad announced that he'd added himself onto the reservation as a special birthday surprise for us. Bex was delighted. It was all "tandem this" and "altitude that" with them. When she asked if I was looking forward to it, I said, 'Hahaha yeah.' I don't think she believed me.

Our pre-jump training instructor, Dave, had the personality of two especially lively golden retrievers rolled into one. I did plan to back out before we got on the plane but somehow his enthusiasm carried me through. The next thing I knew, we were in the sky.

'Nervous?' Bex asked.

'No, I'm excited actually!' my dad replied brightly. Dave, who was strapped to Bex, gave him an approving nod.

'I was asking Livvy,' said Bex.

'A little,' I lied. I don't know why I didn't say what I was thinking. Probably because it could only be expressed in a series of frantic consonants.

'Don't worry!' said Dave, with the usual exclamation mark at the end of his sentence. 'If you don't want to jump, you don't have to! Right, Owen?!'

Owen was my tandem partner. I was already attached to him. In a special dual harness. He was about ten foot tall and the width of a particularly chunky horse. I felt like a safety pin, fastened to the front of his enormous chest. I could feel him nodding his head at Dave's question. 'Yes, jump,' he said. When I asked afterwards if Owen was maybe clinically deaf, Dave assured me that he could hear perfectly.

'He does have a very serious case of selective hearing, though.'

'Why don't you go first, Liv?' Bex suggested. 'Get it over with.'

'Good idea!' said Dave. 'You good to go first, Owen?!'

'Sure!' said Owen brightly. 'I love going first. Always so excited to get going.'

When it came to the actual jumping part, I would like you to know that I did try to say "no." In fact, I did more than try.

'You ready?' Owen asked.

'Not at all,' I replied.

'Great,' said Owen. 'Just walk over to the door.'

I did not walk to the door. *We* walked to the door. I tried to stay rooted where I was. Owen tried to walk towards the ten thousand foot drop to the earth. Owen was about fifty times bigger than me. Owen won. We approached the door. The wind was rushing through my hair. I got a look down. I was absolutely certain I would be backing out right now.

'Ready to jump?' asked Owen.

'No!' I screamed.

'Go?' said Owen. 'Ok!'

And "we" jumped from a plane like maniacs.

Believe me when I say I screamed the whole way down.

The only good thing about the whole ordeal was seeing my family's faces as they landed. My dad was first. He was ashen. He rushed into my arms and hugged me like he'd thought he would never see me again. 'Oh, Liv,' he said. 'Never again!' I couldn't agree more. I wanted to, but he was holding me so tightly against him that I couldn't talk.

'Again?' asked Owen.

Bex was a different story. She was radiant. She ran over to us as soon as she landed, dragging along Dave who was still attached to her. Dave didn't seem to mind too much, if the way he wooped was anything to go by. She threw her arms about both of us. 'Again! Again!'

'Again!' repeated Dave happily. 'But not today! You only paid for one session! Do you want to book another?!'

'No,' I said quickly.

'Not if my life depended on it,' said my dad.

Poor Dave looked crestfallen, until Liv gave him her best smile and said, 'Yes, please!'

For years to come, Bex would refer to this as "our best birthday" and I didn't even bother to correct her. I didn't like sky diving. I'd rather have all my teeth pulled than go sky diving again. But I always thought of Bex's smile. Bex needed to jump out of planes and kiss boys and drink with her friends to find happiness. I didn't need any of that. I just needed the people I loved happy. I just needed Bex to smile like that. I just needed Bex to be ok.

Friday – The Eulogy

'Hello earthlings!' Luna's voice startled me awake. 'Don't worry, this isn't about the pesky missile we just had to shoot down. I have to say I didn't have "Switzerland tries to nuke the Government of the Known-Universe" on my end of the world bingo card. Did you? Max Smith, we would like you to know that we have voted just now and we unanimously agree that missiles do fall under your remit. So please, for the love of god, get it together!'

Through the wall, I heard Max's wife say, 'For goodness sake, Max. You couldn't even stop Switzerland? Switzerland!'

'I know, I know.' Max sounded like he'd aged ten years since Sunday. I was a bit jealous, to be honest. I wouldn't have minded having ten more years. 'I'm trying.'

Shine appeared in my doorway, rubbing his eyes. What was it about him half-asleep, still wearing the black robe, that made me want to jump his bones? 'Is this the Eulogy?' he asked.

'The what?'

'Anyway, it's time for the Eulogy!' said Luna cheerily. 'Our gracious Deputy PM, Sol the First, is letting me do this one all by myself, since I'm a bit of an Earth buff. Isn't that exciting?'

'Couldn't care less!' shouted a harried Max from next door.

'Max Smith, I am warning you. You are on very thin ice already today.'

'Sorry!' Max piped up, and shifted his focus back to his laptop. With his two index fingers, and intense focus, he typed "*contact details world leaders*" into Google.

'So, for anyone who doesn't know,' Luna continued. 'The Eulogy is a time-honoured tradition of planet-wide extinction events. This is what will go into the Intergalactic Archives. Whenever anyone wants to know something about your planet, it will be there for them to find. Isn't that fun?'

'Yes! So fun!' said Max.

'Thank you, Max Smith,' said Luna. 'But you won't butter me up that easily. So, without further ado, here is the Eulogy for Earth.' Luna cleared her throat and it sounded like snails climbing up a wall.

'Citizens of Earth, I cannot express in words how difficult it has been for us to come to the decision to end your planet since we found out about your disease a week ago. This truly is the bitterest of goodbyes. We barely had the chance to know you, and you had none at all to know us. We are truly sorry that you got the raw end of the deal.'

'As you all likely know, Earth was initially populated several million years ago by the Eih-Nor, a species that would eventually go on to flourish in the greater universe. Upon hearing the news that the Earth was set for destruction, the leader of the Eih-Nor was quoted saying, "Where?" And then, when one of my esteemed colleagues enlightened him, he said, "Oh, that expletive expletive expletive in the middle of nowhere." Which we all thought was a touching tribute. You'd think so too if you knew the kinds of things the Eih-Nor say about the Government of the Known-Universe. I don't mind sharing that my feelings have been hurt on more than one occasion. Quite hurt. You'd think they were the ones running…'

I could practically hear her shaking herself. 'Sorry, sorry, this is about Earth, not me. The Eih-Nor settled primarily in a place that is now known as Manchester.' She rolled the "r" at least a dozen times. 'Am I saying that right? Manchesterrrrrrr.' She rolled the "r" even more. 'I suppose it doesn't matter. It'll be gone soon. Anyway, the Eih-Nor quickly found that there was just far too much rain to make it a habitable place for any species. Or, as they called it, "expletive expletive sky water." So they left, but not before they went around the world setting up "dinosaur" skeletons as a practical joke. That's right, everyone! The conspiracy theorists were right all along. Well, except for the fact that evolution is real and Earth is not flat and don't get me started on the moon landings, as if you actually have a moon…

'Sorry, sorry. You don't need to hear about that again. The point is, the Eih-Nor left. Humans eventually evolved from chickens. You know the rest, bringing us to the beautiful, thriving world we have today, which we are about to blow up. Sorry again for all your losses.

'But, hey, who wants to hear some fun Earth stats?'

No one responded.

'I can't hear you!'

'Weeyyy!' called next door's teenager, Lily, who had returned from the circus after setting a bunch of lions free.

'Thank you, Lily Smith, daughter of the Representative of Earth,' said Luna. 'Your enthusiasm is appreciated. So let's get started! And what better place to begin than war. Big shoutout to Britain for having the most wars of any country, coming in strong with over 120, maybe even 150. Gosh your research tools are a minefield! And that's only counting the ones since the Act of Union in 1707. Impressive.'

There were cheers. I heard several people shout. 'England! England! England!' I buried my face in my hands.

'But Poland, you weren't far behind with 105. Who'd have thought it? And, depending on who you ask, it might even be up to 200. You're lucky I don't really understand the internet, Britain. While we're on the topic of war, I ought to give an honorary mention to Sweden and Denmark for most wars fought against the same opponents. Twenty-seven. You guys must really hate each other!'

I heard a lone voice cheering and shouting, 'Sverige! Sverige!'

'And if we want to talk about who has done the most science, that would be the United States of America. You guys make so many scientific discoveries it's not even funny. Actually, it's a little funny, since it's all going to mean nothing in a few days.' There was that rattling raisin-waterfall laugh again. 'Sorry, I crack myself up.'

She went on like this for a while, listing countries and their achievements. Everything from the most beautiful fjords, to the most skateboards, to the silliest dogs, to greatest distrust in cheese.

She wrapped up with, 'But, for all the differences that all your arbitrarily defined countries have, you do have something in common…'

I waited for her to say something cheesy about humanity and connection.

'We would all prefer you didn't blow us up into a million pieces?' asked Max next door.

'I was going to say you're all going to be dead in two days, but that works too,' said Luna brightly. 'Well, that was the Eulogy. I'm going to hold for applause now.'

She held a long time. Eventually, we all gave in and clapped for her.

'Oh, all that applause for me? I'm touched, Earth. But not touched enough not to murder you all. Anyway, that's it for now. I'll be back again in a couple of days to announce the end. Max Smith, please stay on the line. We need to have words. Toodaloo everyone else!'

'Well, that was weird,' I said when the tannoy went off. Shine grinned. He definitely had too many teeth. He seemed to realise it at the same time I did, since a few of them disappeared. I checked my watch. Six fifteen am. I sighed. 'Can't even get a lie in at the apocalypse. We're up now, so cuppa and a slice of toast? I stole some of the cheap white bread you liked.'

'Not today, Liv.'

'But...'

'Save your appetite. Trust me on this one.'

Friday – Not about the food

The final days of Amandeep Singh – Mumbai, India

My first thought was that I had never seen so many people packed into one room. My second thought was how hungry I was.

'Eat, eat,' commanded an older lady wearing a yellow sari.

'Padma aunty,' said Amandeep, the object of Shine's study. He had a little boy on his lap and was eating some mouth-watering curry. 'Why did you let these people into the house? We don't know them?'

'Who cares about that,' said Padma. 'It's the end of the world. Everyone should be eating.'

'Yes, but do they have to be eating our food?' asked Amandeep.

Padma looked at him as if he was crazy. 'Yes,' she said.

'Aunty, I really do think…'

'Where are you from?' she asked us, cutting off Amandeep.

Shine remained silent and I said, 'England.'

'There you go!' Padma said, staring pointedly at Amandeep. 'England. Do you want to deny this poor child a chance to have the only good food she'll ever eat? And this one's all skin and bones.' She jerked a thumb at Shine. 'Now Amandeep Singh, you're going to stop scowling and enjoy the meal.' She looked back at me and Shine. 'Eat,' she urged us.

'Can I have some of that bread?' asked the little boy on Amandeep's knee. He was pointing to a bread-based dish a little girl was holding. It was identical to the one in his own hand.

'No, it's mine,' said the little girl. The boy tried to snatch for it and the girl squealed, 'Gi' o'r!'

Under Padma's firm stare, Amandeep sighed and said, 'Please help yourselves. What is mine is apparently yours.' The older lady elbowed him. 'Sorry, aunty. You are welcome guests in our home.'

Shine did not need any more encouragement than that. He dug in, sampling everything in front of him with grunts of appreciation. I was a little more uncertain. It was quite clear that Amandeep didn't really want us here, and I wasn't used to eating with my hands. All my doubts disappeared the second I tasted the food. It was some kind of chickpea curry with fried bread and it was divine.

'Oh my god, this is so good!'

'See,' Padma said to Amandeep. 'She likes the chicken tikka masala.'

'Of course she does, Padma aunty. It's delicious. That wasn't the point I was trying to...' Amandeep sighed and shook his head.

'This doesn't taste much like chicken tikka masala,' I muttered to Shine. 'For one thing, there's no chicken in it.'

'Oh, it's the ruddy interpreter again!' Shine grumbled, tapping the side of his head as if it would help. 'It's doing its whole creative license thing, "translating" what she actually said into something British for you.'

'And it picked chicken tikka masala?'

'Of course. It was invented in the UK. You should know that, Liv! That's your culture. Anyway what's more British than a cheeky curry after a night out?'

'How do you know about cheeky curries and nights out, Shine?'

'Research,' he said. I wasn't sure what kind of research exactly and I got the impression he didn't want me to ask because he crammed "chicken tikka masala" into his mouth like nobody's business. Through his mouthful of food, he proceeded to ask, 'So who is everybody? Are you all family?'

'In the loosest possible definition of the word,' replied Amandeep.

Padma tutted at him. 'We are family,' she insisted. 'All of us. Aunties and uncles and cousins and grandparents and children and grandchildren and every kind of family you can imagine. It's not my fault you don't take the time to get to know your cousins.'

'Yes, aunty,' said Amandeep but he was laughing, and I could see the love there. It made me happy for him in a way that left me wanting to get down on the floor, roll up into a ball and cry until the end of the world.

I didn't think anyone could have noticed, because I'd done such a good job of forcing a smile onto my face and nodding my head in interest. I was surprised when Shine reached under the table and took my hand.

'And you will spend the end of the world like this? Eating?' Even as he continued with his questions, his hand held mine. Steadying me with its continual warmth. It made it a bit harder to eat, but I didn't mind.

Padma opened her mouth again but Amandeep got there first. 'It's not really about the eating. It's about who we're eating with.'

'Is that so?' asked Shine, shovelling a chunk of bread and curry into his mouth. The little boy on Amandeep's lap was looking at him suspiciously.

'See that beautiful woman over there.' Amandeep said, pointing to an admittedly gorgeous lady in a long flowing dress. 'I knew from the moment I met her that she would be the love of my life.'

'Because she is what I believe is called a hottie?' asked Shine, as the little boy reached over to poke his face. The child leapt back, staring at the alien accusingly.

Amandeep looked angry for a second and then he shrugged. 'Not just that, because she was so fierce. Some kids had found a stray dog and were bothering it with sticks. It was cruel. I was going to say something, but she laid into them. I have never seen anything so lovely as her rage. I still have a hard time believing she married me.' He pointed to the little boy, who was still staring at Shine. 'Or that we have such a spirited little monster.' He held his arms wide. 'And as for the rest of these busybodies…'

'Watch what you say!' Padma interrupted him. 'Busybodies indeed!'

'I just can't think of a better way to go out than eating a good meal with a good family, can you?'

I couldn't answer. There was a lump stuck in my throat like I'd tried to eat too fast, which I had but I didn't think that was the reason. Shine squeezed my hand softly. He grounded me.

Amandeep's wife came over and draped an arm over his shoulder. 'Don't say that, love,' she scolded him. I saw some of that fire in her eyes. 'Your aunties have always been good to you.'

'Yes, dear,' said Amandeep, kissing her hand. 'You are right, as always.'

They were such a lovely couple. I admired their every touch. My panic was spreading from my stomach to my fingertips. I held on to Shine for dear life.

'He's wrong anyway,' said Padma.

'I know, aunty. I'm sorry. You're not busybodies.'

Some of the rage in his wife's eyes cooled. She ran her fingers through his hair. It looked like she'd done it so many times that I doubted she was even aware of it. I was. I was so aware of it. And I was even more aware when Shine lifted his hand to my head and patted me rhythmically. It was a strange feeling, warm currents running down my scalp with every touch like I was in the shower. It also was a decidedly inhuman gesture. Mainly because he made a third arm to do it. But it made me feel a little less alone.

'Not about the busybody thing!' Padma said. 'Who cares about that? Besides, you need some busibodying sometimes! You'd never have plucked up the courage to ask Tavleen to marry you if I didn't tell her cousin's best friend that you thought she was gorgeous.'

'True,' Amandeep acknowledged. 'Although, you did break my trust when you did that.'

Padma snorted. 'Someone had to, didn't they, love? Anyway, let's not talk about who did or didn't spend several years creating false dating profiles for her nephew.'

'Aunty did you…?'

'I said let's not talk about that! Do you have ears, boy? Anyway, it didn't matter because there were no takers.' She saw Amandeep's hurt look and doubled down. 'What? Would you want there to be takers? You ended up with Tavleen. Look at her. She's way out of your league!'

Amandeep didn't seem to mind that. He smiled at his wife. 'She is,' he agreed. 'But, go on then, what was I wrong about?'

'You said it's not about the food. To think, a nephew of mine expressing such a foolish opinion! It *is* all about the food.' And lively debate started up around us while I felt as if I was sinking.

Later, back in my little house, Shine put his arms about me. I wondered if aliens normally gave hugs, or if he'd picked it up while he was here, but either way it was what I needed. I snuggled against him.

'I think I've done everything wrong,' I whispered.

'There is more than one way to live, Liv,' Shine replied.

'But that was the right one, wasn't it?'

'There is no right or wrong,' Shine told me. 'But it's ok if that's the way you wish you were spending these days. It's ok if that's what you want.'

I nodded against his chest. 'I wish I'd foreseen the alien apocalypse and filled my life with friends and family and tried harder to fall in love. I never even considered that I was setting myself up to die alone. I always thought... I always thought I'd have...'

'Bex?' he asked softly. 'And your dad?' All I could do was nod.

Shine broke away from me. He took my face in his hands and looked into my eyes. His were now purple with little flecks of gold. 'If it helps, you won't be alone at the end. You'll be with me. And we might even get to go out watching quiz shows together. Wouldn't that be lovely?'

Despite the fact that my heart felt like a ship's anchor, I couldn't help but say, 'Yes. Yes it would.' And then he was cuddling me again.

'Liv?'

'Mm?'

'Am I still beautiful to you?'

I couldn't understand why he kept asking that bloody question. 'Yes,' I sighed. 'You are still what humans call a "hottie."'

He laughed and my frustration faded a little. 'Sorry.' Then, with cheeks that turned red as tomatoes, he added, 'Just so you know, you're a hottie too.'

The wrong bin

The history of Liv and Bex

I was what I liked to call perpetually single. I wasn't a nun. I didn't have the face for a wimple. I went on dates, usually with guys Bex set me up with. Ambitious medical students or doctors who thought I was cute but who, on the whole, would rather have dated my sister. Occasionally, the date would lead us back to his place. Then, the next morning, we'd realise we had nothing in common.

'I don't think you're even trying, Livvy,' Bex complained after a two-week romance with one of her doctor friends.

'I am,' I lied. 'It's just, they don't want to date a call centre worker. They don't know what to say to me. I'm not as cool as them.'

Bex squared up to me. 'Don't talk about my sister that way!'

'It's not like you're any different,' I said, exasperated. 'You're not going out of your way to date the binman or something.' I felt bad as soon as I said it. Bex wasn't an elitist. She just didn't really date anyone. It had been three years since she broke up with John and, other than that disastrous little interlude with Fred, there hadn't really been anyone else. 'I'm sorry, Bex. I didn't mean that, I just…'

'No, you're right,' said Bex thoughtfully. 'The binman is quite cute, actually.'

The truth was that Bex thought he was more than cute. She thought he was what Shine would have called a hottie. She'd noticed him about a month before this conversation and once she did notice him, she couldn't stop thinking about him.

She had been on night shifts at the hospital, and made an effort to complain about them as much as possible. She drafted an email to the director of her training programme as a joke.

Dear (look the name up later),

I'll have you know that I decided to be a GP precisely because I want normal working hours. I can't be doing with night shifts, truth be told. They're an affront to nature.

As a doctor, I'm sure I don't need to tell you about circadian/circadien (sp?) rhythm or homeostatic sleep drive. It is virtually impossible for me to sleep during the day and I'm <u>DYING</u> here. I am so tired that I can't tell a liver from a lover (change this to kidney if you ever actually send this to make a better point).

131.

Kindly explain to me why it is so necessary for me to do hospital placements. Especially Accident and Emergency. Everyone knows that people go to A&E when they should go to their GP, not the other way round.

Overall, I think the NHS would be a better place if I could just get a good night's sleep.

Thanks in advance for cancelling my night shifts! Rebecca Olivia Waller

Bex was laughing so hard at the part about A&E, that she accidentally clicked send. There was a moment of horror when she noticed what she had done. Then she cheered up when she realised there was a non-zero chance this ended in her getting off the night shift.

Her hopes were to be dashed mere hours later.

Dear Rebecca Olivia Waller,

I am afraid that hospital placements are essential to the training programme. Please kindly refer to your common sense to figure out why it might be useful for a GP to be able to recognise a broken leg. I have checked your schedule and you are on nights for three weeks. I sympathise with your lovers but hopefully they can wait that long for you to recognise them again.

Yours sincerely,

Look the name up later (aka Patrick Chambers – you had to search my name in your inbox to find who to send the email to so I think you were just being rude with this)

So it was that Bex was stuck in a perpetual state of grumpy tiredness, completely unable to function. On Wednesday morning, when she arrived back from shift, she saw the bins out on her street and cursed. She'd meant to put it out before going on shift. Why did so much of adulthood seem to consist of putting bins out when you wanted to be in bed? Half-asleep, she put out the green one and curled up under her duvet to snore away in an undignified fashion.

She awoke to the Armageddon of the bin world. The Johnny-come-latelys hadn't been sure whether to trust Bex or the rest of the street. Even some of the people who'd put their bins out the night before had been thrown.

'It's blue bin week, isn't it? Did they change the schedule? No one bloody tells me anything around here!'

'It's definitely blue bin. Leave it, Andy. I said leave it!'

'I'm not getting caught out if it's green. It's almost full and I can't wait another two weeks.'

'We'll just put stuff in my mum's bin if we have to. Not that we'll have to, since it's definitely blue!'

'Are you having a laugh? Haven't you noticed how protective your mum's been over her bins lately? I'm not getting into it with her again over an old bean bag chair. I'm already the least favourite son-in-law. She's told me that before. I know how to pick my battles. Nope, I'm putting out green.'

'But it's not green, Andy!'

'Well, someone clearly knows something we don't.'

By the time the bin lorry arrived in the mid-afternoon, the neighbourhood was divided, half and half. People were anxiously staring from their windows. Andy's whole marriage was riding on this.

Bex emerged from her house just in time to see the last blue bin being emptied.

'Oh no!' she cried, thinking of all of the cardboard boxes she was going to have to fly tip now.

134.

Then the binman turned around to look at her. He was young, her age or there abouts, with dark hair and eyelashes she'd have dreams about in the coming weeks. He was about to tell her better luck next time, but then he saw her. And he realised he couldn't. He always maintained it was how tired and stricken she looked. Bex's friend Katie would later playfully nudge him in the ribs and say, 'Come on, you just fancied her, didn't you?'

He would blush and say, 'Well, *obviously.* But I wasn't risking a disciplinary over someone just because I thought she was hot.'

He obviously was, but that's not important now. What matters is that he saw my sister with her hands over her mouth and smiled. 'Quickly,' he said. 'Go get your blue one.'

'Paul, lad, we're on a schedule,' protested his colleague, as Bex ran into the garden. Paul insisted that they wait for her. He got into so much trouble for that. Since they ended up getting married, I'm guessing he thought it was worth it.

'So sorry!' she said. 'I'm a doctor and I'm working nights. I'm such an idiot right now. I put out the wrong one. Oh dear, a lot of people copied me, didn't they?'

'No problem, love,' said Paul as he emptied the bin into the lorry. Then he leaned closer to her and whispered. 'I love it when this happens. It's my favourite kind of chaos. We best be off before any of your neighbours notice.' He winked at her and the lorry set off again, slowly ambling away as it was chased by a crowd of angry neighbours, pointing at blue bins they'd brought out last minute. A chorus of livid voices surrounded Bex.

The man from forty-three said, 'I knew it was too good to be true! Two green bin weeks in a row. That never happens, does it? But I wanted to believe. I needed to believe in something this week after I got fired and my cat went missing and my girlfriend left me to start a life as a celebrity look-alike in Dundee.'

The woman from thirty-nine said, 'Did you see they let forty-two rush back for hers? Never in my life have I seen such blatant favouritism. I'll be writing a letter to the council!'

'You do that, Angela. At some point they're going to have to start taking all your complaints seriously. How many is it now?'

'Coming up on thirty-one.'

And, of course, the couple at thirty-five started divorce proceedings. 'I *told* you it was blue, Andy. Why wouldn't you listen? My mum was right. I would have been better off marrying Bob!'

Bex didn't care. She was thinking about dark eyes and long eyelashes and a wink that made her feel things she hadn't in years.

136.

The next two Wednesdays, she couldn't help herself. She rushed out of the house whenever she heard the bin lorry. Her reasons were tenuous at best. The first time, she pretended that she wanted to be doubly sure she'd put the right bin out. She felt like an idiot, as she made a pantomime of looking at all the bins on the street and nodding to herself. Then Paul the binman waved at her and her heart fluttered, and it felt like a good decision. The second time, she pretended to be looking for an earring. Only after she got back into the house did she realise that her ears weren't pierced.

'Well, I could have lost someone else's earring,' she told herself indignantly.

The following week, she was back on day shifts, but she found herself thinking about Paul's arms as she listened to a woman's heart. 'This is no good,' she scolded herself.

'What is no good?' asked the woman nervously. 'Is it my heart? I wasn't even here for medical attention and now I'm dying!'

Bex blinked at her. 'You weren't? What were you here for then?'

'It's actually my first day on the job as a trainee nurse.'

'Then why am I listening to your heart?'

'I'm not sure,' said the woman, blinking very fast. 'I did think it was strange. What with us being in the canteen and everything.'

Bex looked about her and cursed. 'This is really no good,' she grumbled, and wandered away thinking about Paul's eyes as the poor woman begged everyone around her to listen to her heart.

After I made my snide little comment about the binman, Bex realised she couldn't pass up the opportunity anymore. She called work the following Wednesday morning. 'I couldn't possibly come in today,' she rasped and faked a cough for good measure.

'Are you sure?' asked her boss. 'It's Maria's birthday and there's cake.'

That gave Bex pause, but only for a second. 'No, sorry. I'm still ill.'

'Good,' said her boss approvingly. She had passed the cake test. 'Hope you feel better soon!'

This time when the bin lorry arrived, Bex was brave. 'Do you want to go out with me some time?'

Paul's eyes widened. 'Me?'

'She's not talking to me, is she, lad?' guffawed his colleague. He was in his late fifties with a grey mullet. 'Don't just stand there like an idiot. Get her number and get back on task.'

The way Paul scrambled for his phone made my sister feel all kinds of happy.

'Dozy bugger,' said the other binman in a way that suggested he thought of Paul almost as a son.

They met at a nice restaurant three days later. Paul was wearing a suit with a powder blue tie. Bex was in a red dress. When he saw her, his jaw practically dropped to the ground.

'You look so handsome,' she said, never one to keep her compliments to herself.

'You... um... wow! I mean, wow!'

He was tongue tied for the first hour or so, but she thought that was adorable. She was happy to natter on about work and religion and the world and us.

'So you have another half,' said Paul when she spoke about me. 'Literally.'

Bex laughed. I don't think she ever really knew what impact her laugh had on people, especially Paul. He melted for her every single time. 'That's actually not exactly how twins work. I mean, not for me and Liv anyway. It's really interesting actually, if you...' Her voice trailed away. 'Oh, sorry. I didn't mean to correct you.'

'No, please do,' he urged. 'I don't mind being wrong if I get to learn new things. What were you going to say?'

And now Bex almost felt like crying. This is what she had been missing. She reached towards him across the table and laced her fingers through his.

'Well, if we were identical twins then we would have formed from a single egg splitting, and I guess you could say we were two halves of the same person. But we aren't. We're fraternal twins, which means we were two separate eggs who happened to get fertilised at the same time. Sorry, is that boring?'

'Not at all,' Paul assured her. 'Is it true that twins have a genetic component? Are there more twins in your family history?' And as she explained, he stared at her with hearts for eyes.

I'm sure you can tell by now that Paul was completely besotted with Bex. He wasn't an idiot. He knew how absolutely out of his league she was. He assumed that all he would get with her was one date. She was bound to realise she could do better. He didn't even care. He knew he'd always remember this as the best day of his life. He hung on her every word.

He almost choked on his coffee when they asked for the bill and she said, 'I wish this didn't have to end.'

'Me too! My parents didn't even believe me when I said I was going out with a beautiful doctor.'

'You told your parents about me?'

'I hope that's ok?' Paul asked, bright red. 'I wasn't weird or anything. I'm just close to my family and I was excited about this date.'

Bex was beaming. 'I told my family too. My dad wants to interrogate you at some point. Don't worry, he only actually uses the kitchen knife for chopping veg. He just thinks it's really funny to scare the boys I date.'

'Do you... Do you want to continue the date? We could go to a bar and, um, well...'

'Make out a bunch?' she suggested with a wicked grin.

Paul nodded vigorously. 'Yes, please!' And he decided to start the night early, leaning across the table to kiss her. Bex was in heaven.

The rest was history. They fell in love, a deeper, happier love than she'd had with John. She didn't just light up around Paul. She glowed.

Paul was a little nervous to meet us. He was worried we wouldn't think he was good enough. *He* didn't think he was good enough. He counted his lucky stars every day that Rebecca Waller had once put the wrong bin out.

He needn't have worried. We'd liked John but we *loved* Paul. We didn't care what his job was. We cared that he looked at Bex like she hung the moon. He never took her for granted. He saw Bex the way she had been waiting her whole life for someone to see her.

The first time we met him, we could barely contain our opinions. As soon as Paul nipped to the loo, we bombarded Bex.

'He's so lovely!' I said. 'I loved the way he was all gooey when you went off on that rant about the patriarchy. He really seemed to be open to burning it down to the ground and he didn't look scared at all.'

'Such a nice lad,' my dad agreed. 'Don't know what he's doing with you.'

'Daddy!' Bex shrieked, but she was laughing.

'I like him,' my dad mollified her. 'I do.'

'You don't think he's a surface person?' Bex picked at her cuticle. 'I don't have the best history of spotting those.'

'Not at all. He has more depth in his little finger than John had in his whole body. He knows what he has in you. I like that.'

Now, Paul just so happened to hear most of this conversation and his heart was absolutely full. That didn't even change when my dad said, 'I'm still going to try and scare him by asking about his intentions with my daughter, though.' He sounded very proud of himself.

And so, when my dad did ask this, after Paul returned to the living room, my sister's boyfriend was ready. 'That's easy, I want to marry her and have twelve children.' At the shock on everyone's faces, he burst out laughing. 'Kidding. About the twelve children. I do want to marry her one day, though. Got to lock down the best thing that I've ever had before she notices I collect rubbish for a living.'

Bex laughed and kissed him fully. 'I would marry you in a heartbeat,' she said. 'I would marry you in the bin lorry if you needed me to.'

'That's lovely, Bex.'

'But, Bexy, why would he need that?' I asked.

She shrugged. 'You never know.'

'That's right,' echoed Paul. 'You never know.'

When they did get married, a year and a half later, it wasn't in a bin lorry. Although Bex made enough jokes about it that we all started to get worried. What she really wanted was twenty-three ceremonies, one for each of her religions. Paul would have gone along with it, but my dad put his foot down.

'That daft lad's too in love with you to see sense.'

'He is, isn't he?' said Bex dreamily.

My dad was horrified. He hadn't meant her to take it as a compliment. He tried a different tactic. 'You can't expect people to sit through all that religious nonsense, Bex. Pick your favourite.'

'But dad,' Bex protested. 'I can't do that. It's like asking you to pick your favourite child.'

'That's easy right now,' said my dad. 'Liv.'

'Daddy!' Bex was aghast.

'Well, she's not planning to torture me with a thirty minute ceremony entirely in Japanese for starters.'

In the end, after much umming and ahing and cursing my dad's name, Bex picked a Quaker ceremony. She described it as her first love. Then, with a teasing smile, 'That's probably why daddy loves you best. You came first.'

'Only by a few minutes!'

I didn't bother to correct her because we both knew our dad genuinely didn't have a favourite. He loved us equally, just as we were.

Despite my dad's ongoing reservations, it was a lovely wedding. Bex was bright and beautiful as she walked down the aisle in her lace dress. Paul cried. Paul cried a lot. She cried a bit too. Paul's parents couldn't stop telling us about how much they loved her. How astonished they were about their son's luck, and how happy they were for our families to merge.

Late in the night, while we were dancing to some cheesy pop music, I said to Bex, 'It's been such a wonderful day.'

'I know,' she replied. 'I'm so happy I could burst.'

But the thing was, it was only a half truth. She was happy. She was the happiest she'd ever been. And, still, even as Paul appeared, grabbing her hands and spinning her round and round making her giggle, she was still the little girl from the pillow fort. She was still trying. She was always trying.

Until she wasn't.

Saturday – Power cuts

The final days of Maria Micaela Brondino – Cordoba, Argentina

Shine and I were standing outside a perfectly white house and listening to the music that shook the walls.

'Should have brought my earplugs,' I grumbled.

'What?' said Shine and laughed at his own joke. 'You aren't laughing, Liv?'

'I've just heard that one before,' I said.

'What?'

'I said, "I've heard…" Goddamn it!'

'If it helps, Liv, many people have fallen for that one before. Over three million people, if my research is correct.'

I did some more grumbling to myself and he leaned over and kissed me on the cheek. If you haven't figured it out by now, there are few things Shine could do that I wouldn't forgive him for if he kissed me on the cheek afterwards.

I wish he hadn't pointed at me and said, 'Liv, you're blushing!' though.

As soon as we knocked at the door, we were dragged inside by a pretty young woman in a strappy top and an inviting smile. 'Come in!'

'You aren't worried about the fact that you don't know us?' I asked.

'What are you going to do? Kill me?' She grinned and made slightly tasteless finger guns with her hands.

'You're Maria, aren't you?' asked Shine.

'Maria!' She laughed. 'Who's Maria?' One unidentifiable bass-heavy song ended and another, almost identical bass-heavy song began. 'This is my tune!' she said and started to dance.

'Maria Micaeala Brondino?' Shine tried again. 'That's who we're looking for and I am relatively certain that is you. I really hope my sensor hasn't broken.' He started hitting himself on the side of the head.

She did a sort of worm like movement with her body. 'You really aren't from here, are you?'

'Not at all,' Shine said happily.

'Everyone is called Maria,' she explained. 'At least in their first name. So no one goes by it. Isn't that how it works where you're from?' She looked at us expectantly.

'I chose my own name,' Shine offered happily.

'That's nice,' she said. 'Anyway, I'm Micaela.' She looked at me and her eyes traced up and down my body. '*You* can call me Mica.'

'Is she flirting with you, Liv?' Shine asked. 'Is it time for me to act like your boyfriend again so that you can roll your eyes and say I'm not your boyfriend? How did I do that before? Was it when I made myself ten feet tall?'

'You don't need to act like my...'

But it was too late. Shine was back in his demon form. '*DON'T UPSET LIV,*' he said in his hellish voice.

'You're not upsetting me,' I assured Mica.

She just smiled and began to dance circles about us both.

'You don't have to pretend to be my boyfriend any time someone shows interest in me,' I told Shine.

Shine shrunk down. 'But then how will they know we're a team?' he asked in a quiet voice.

'They don't need to know we're a team,' I assured him. '*We* know we're a team.'

'That's true!' Shine was bright again. 'So, Micaela, tell me a little bit about the la...' He paused. I realised he was about to talk about her fast approaching death. The fact he was able to stop himself was, frankly, a miracle. I was proud of him. 'This party. Is this your house? Are you with your friends or family?'

'Friends,' she confirmed. 'My family weren't very nice to me.'

'I'm sorry to hear that,' said Shine in that earnest way of his. 'Would you like to talk about your childhood?'

'At a party? No chance, love.' Mica began to spin round and round, her arms in the air. 'Then again, look about you. This is my family. Isn't my family beautiful?'

'Yes,' said Shine.

'Yes,' I repeated. And they were, dancing, eating, drinking. Happy. People of all ages, wearing all kinds of clothes from a tracksuit to a ballgown. I'd never seen a house look so alive.

Mica gave me a sultry look. 'Do you think I'm a good dancer?' she asked.

'Sure,' I said. She was doing the hand jive.

Shine didn't seem pleased about this change of topic. 'So you're just having a big party with everyone you care about?' he clarified.

'Exactly! We have barbeque and alcohol and a pool. And we have tea, of course. Have you tried a cuppa tea?'

I frowned. 'I'm English. We're kind of famous for it.'

Mica's eyes went wide. 'No? I knew we had to argue with other South Americans over who drinks the most cuppas, but I never knew I was meant to argue with you too!'

'Oh, Liv, she's not actually saying cuppas. She's saying cuppas.' Shine cursed. 'This stupid interpreter. You know I'm not actually trying to say cuppas, right?'

'What are you trying to say then?'

'I'll write it down!' Mica ran off to get a sheet of paper. She came back and showed me what she'd written on it. It said, "*Cuppa tea, love?*"

'I'll turn off the interpreting for a second,' Shine said. 'How do I get the bloody…?' Mid way through the sentence his speech turned into a series of bells and wind chime sounds. Everyone about me was suddenly speaking Spanish without Yorkshire accents. It was disconcerting. I looked at the paper in front of me. It now read, "*Mate?*"

I said, 'Yeah, I'll be your mate!'

Mica said a lot of words very fast in Spanish. Then she picked up the paper, tapped it twice and said, 'Maté.' She was pronouncing it wrong, like 'matt-ay.'

I decided to help her out. 'Mate,' I corrected.

She rushed off and came back with a drink with a little round cup with a straw in it. She held it out to me. 'Maté.'

Shine must have switched the interpretation back on. 'It's the name of the drink,' he explained.

'Cuppa tea?' asked Mica.

'Sure.'

150.

Before I had the chance to try it, the lights went out. Someone shouted, 'Power cut!'

'Oh good,' said Mica. 'Kiss me?'

'Uh, ok.'

I was too surprised to do anything but exactly what she asked. A few seconds later the lights came back on and Mica was smiling at me mischievously. 'We're used to power cuts around here but they've been happening even more frequently since the world started ending,' she explained. 'Now whenever there is a power cut, we kiss someone until the lights come back on to make it fun.'

'That was a really short power cut,' Shine observed.

Mica giggled. 'A lot of them aren't really power cuts. People just turn off the lights to have the excuse to make out.' She looked at Shine. 'Sorry I made you the third wheel. I'm just not really into that whole Rotherham Show thing.'

'Rotherham Show? What?'

'Rotherham Show,' repeated Mica, nodding her head.

I thought it through until it dawned on me. 'Shine is she actually saying Carnival?'

'That's right,' Shine confirmed. 'Rotherham Show. Oh for goodness sake. I'll turn it off again hang on…'

'No, it's ok, I got it. He's not wearing a costume. He's just an alien.'

Mica shrugged. 'Not really into aliens either then, I guess. I'm really sorry. No offence meant. You seem perfectly nice except for all this.' She pointed to his entire face and body.

'None at all taken!' Despite Shine's bright tone, he seemed a little down.

'I'm into aliens,' I muttered, mostly to make him feel better.

Shine looked at me, his eyes widening slightly. 'Are you really, Liv?'

Why had I said that? Other than the fact it was true and I'd be dead tomorrow, of course. Did I really want to spend the end of the world humiliated. I took a sip of the drink and made a slight face. It tasted a bit like bitter grass. 'I'm not sure this is for me.'

Mica grinned brightly. 'Thank you,' she said.

'It wasn't a compliment.' I looked at Shine helplessly.

'The interpreter is programmed to avoid certain cultural incidents,' he explained. 'She thinks you said that it's the best drink you ever had in your life. "Better than a cup of tea on a hard day." The same thing would happen if you tried to tell a French person that Brits make better cheese.'

Mica was nodding vigorously in a way that told me she had no idea what he was saying.

I was in the process of opening my mouth to try to communicate to her that I didn't actually like the drink, when the lights went out again.

'Power cut!'

I prepared for Mica to grab me again, but that's not what happened. Shine reached for me instead, his hands on my hips, pulling me towards him. 'Are you really into aliens, Liv?'

I had no idea how to answer that. All I could see in the dark was his glowing hair and the ultraviolet of his irises. I put my arms about his neck. I leaned towards him. 'May I?'

He hesitated. 'It's not allowed.'

'Sorry.' I tried to pull away but he drew me back to him.

'Don't, Liv.'

'But…'

'It's not allowed but…' His voice was sort of gruff and gravelly in a way I hadn't heard it before. 'Screw it. Screw the rules. Kiss me.'

I summoned my courage and did as I was told. It was as if I'd been waiting to do this since the moment I met him in my office. Which, for the record, I had. His lips were warm on mine. There was a whole kaleidoscope of butterflies in my stomach.

Then the lights blinked back on. He broke away from me and I was squinting up at him. And the way he was looking back set off a fire in my heart.

'Not fair!' Mica protested amicably. 'I had to be the third wheel.'

'Sorry,' I said, but Shine's hand was still on the small of my back so I didn't really mean it.

She shrugged. 'To be honest, I've been working my way up to kissing someone special anyway.' She pointed at a man with long curly hair. 'That's Mateo Sottano. I've been in love with him since we were five years old and he stole my egg cup.'

'Why don't you go talk to him,' I suggested, still looking at Shine. 'It's the end of the world after all. Shoot your shot.'

'You're right!' she said determinedly. 'Nice to meet you! Enjoy the cuppa!'

The second she was gone, I poured the drink into a plant pot.

'You might have broken an Argentinian law,' Shine said, in a perfectly serious voice.

'Ahah, really?' Now that it was just the two of us, I was nervous around Shine in a way I hadn't been before. I wasn't used to this. I wasn't used to caring. 'I, um… Well, thank you.'

'What for?'

'For letting me kiss you even though it broke the rules.'

'You're very welcome, Liv.'

'Shall we go back home now or…?'

'We could stay here,' Shine suggested. 'We could dance together.'

I winced. 'I'm terrible at dancing.'

'I refuse to believe that.' He grabbed my hand and spun me under his arm over and over. My skirt fanned out. I thought of Bex's wedding. The way Paul had spun her. I looked over at Mica, dancing with the boy she liked. She threw her head back in wild laughter. I felt my smile slipping. 'Something is bothering you,' said Shine. 'Is it me? Did I do something wrong? Liv, what did I do wrong?'

'No, it's not you,' I assured him. 'You're perfect. I just can't believe that everyone we've visited seems so…'

'Happy?' he finished.

'Yes. Shouldn't they be terrified?'

'Are *you* terrified?'

No, I wasn't, but it was different for me.

It was as if Shine read it in my mind. 'I'm glad you're not afraid,' he said. 'I am not glad for the reasons that have taken your fear. But none of that has to matter, Liv. We still have tonight.'

'Why did you ask me to come with you?' I asked. 'Back in the office. Were you trying to help me? Did I look pathetic?'

'No.' Shine stopped dancing in favour of staring at me intensely. 'Not at all! It was because you called me beautiful. That made me happy. I couldn't believe someone as wonderful as you would look at me that way.'

'Are you allowed to think I'm wonderful?'

'No,' he said, but he didn't seem to be going through a crisis of confidence like usual. 'I'm not allowed to feel unhappy when I see you kissing someone else either. But I did, Liv. I felt very unhappy watching Maria Micaela Brondino do what I wanted to do more than anything.'

The lights went out again. Screams of "power cut!" filled the house. This time, instead of me kissing Shine, he kissed me. He kissed me a lot. He kissed me in a way that probably did mean that he was bad at his job.

When the lights came back on, I realised we were floating. Not just him but me too. He was still kissing me, and showed no signs of stopping. His hands were everywhere. Not like that. Get your mind out of the gutter. They were on my face and in my hands, across my arms and my back, as if he wanted to touch every part of me. When he finally broke his lips from mine, he didn't put me down and we didn't stop floating. I expected all eyes to be on us but we scarcely got a second glance. I suppose the barrier for what is normal expands when there's less than twenty-four hours left until the end.

'You really are so beautiful, Liv,' he told me, making little goosebumps grow on my arms. 'I didn't know how beautiful people could be until I met you.'

'I'm sure *that* must be against the rules.'

He put a finger to my lips. 'Our secret,' he whispered. And then he kissed where his finger had been. 'Do you still think I'm beautiful too?'

'More than ever.'

And he smiled, too wide for it to be human.

'It's weird how into you I am after six days,' I mused.

'It's not weird at all. Bex knew the first time she met Paul that he was special.'

'That's true. Of course, she thought John was special too.' I frowned. 'Did I tell you that?'

He shook his head. 'I may have researched you.'

'You know, under any other circumstances I might be forgiven for thinking that's a bit stalkery.'

Shine winced. 'I know. I'm sorry. I had to.'

'Why?'

He didn't answer me. He looked sad. I don't think I'd ever seen him sad before.

'Shine? What is it?'

'It's who we're visiting tomorrow,' he said.

And he told me. And I was so heart-broken and so grateful all at once.

Sunday – Bumblebee

I called Paul the morning of day the world ended. I told him about our plans. I asked if he wanted to be there.

'I can't,' he said. 'I'm sorry. I've said goodbye. I can't be there at the end. I'm not as strong as you.'

'It's ok,' I said. 'You loved her so much while she was herself. That matters most.'

We cried together for a little bit over the phone, and we talked about Bex. How much both of us wished things had been different. Then he said, 'I don't want you to be alone. If you need me, I'll be with you.'

'I won't be alone,' I assured him. 'Shine will be there.'

'What on earth is Shine?'

'My alien boyfriend,' I explained.

'Am I your boyfriend?' Shine asked. He floated around me in a happy little circle.

'Kept that one quiet, didn't you, Livs?' Paul teased.

'It's new. Very new. End of the world new.'

'Is that so? I can't believe it! Livvy Waller spending the end of the world getting it on with an alien.'

'Paul!' I squealed.

'Am I wrong?'

In my embarrassment I said something stupid. 'Please! You know you'd be spending the end of the world with a hot alien too, if you could.' Even as I spoke, it sounded wrong. There hadn't been anyone for Paul after Bex.

Fortunately, he wasn't so easy to offend. 'I should be so lucky! No, I've got grander plans. We've stolen the bin lorry, powered it with rockets and we're going to try and drive it into space.'

'Really?'

Paul snorted. 'No. I'm at home with my parents. We're going to watch a quiz show.'

'Did he say a quiz show? Tell him I love quiz shows!'

'My alien boyfriend would like you to know he approves of your end of the world entertainment.'

He chuckled. 'Alien boyfriend?' he repeated to himself. I could almost hear him shaking his head. 'God, Bex would have loved that for you.' And he was right. She would have. 'I missed you, Liv. I tried to call you. A lot, actually. I wished you'd stayed in touch.'

It hit me harder than I thought it would. 'Me too. I should have. I just… I just didn't know how.'

'It's ok. I'm glad I'm hearing from you now, one last time.'

It seemed like time to say goodbye but I didn't want to. I didn't know it would be so hard. 'I know that Bex told you once that we weren't technically halves of the same person,' I blurted out.

'That was our first date. She told you about that?'

'In detail. She was so excited. She felt so lucky to have met you.'

'I was the lucky one,' Paul said quietly. 'I still think I'm lucky. It wasn't nearly long enough, but how many people get to love someone like Bex. She is the last person I'm ever going to love and that makes me…' He struggled to finish the sentence.

'Happy sad?' I suggested.

Paul laughed. 'Yeah. Really happy sad. Sorry I derailed you. You were talking about not being half her.'

'That's the thing. I was going to say she was wrong. She was my other half. She *is* my other half.'

There was a pause. Then Paul said, 'I know. She's mine too.'

When we eventually hung up, Shine gave me a big hug.

'What's this for?'

He took a while to say something and, when he did, he said, 'Everything.' Which was very nice but didn't answer my question at all.

'When do we need to be there today?' I asked.

He didn't let go of me. I think he might have been sniffing my hair. I wasn't as freaked out by that as I should have been. 'Whenever you're ready.'

That was the problem. I couldn't imagine being ready.

'You know, you don't have to do this,' said Shine into my hair. 'We can stay here. We can put on the same quiz show that lovely Paul will be watching and try to get more answers right than him.'

'Tempting.'

'Or… we can practice kissing.' He shuffled about shyly.

I lifted my face from his chest and pressed my mouth to his. His lips moved against mine instinctively. I arched towards him as his hands gripped me. We melted into it, into each other.

'Sorry,' I said. 'I don't think you need practice.'

'What a ridiculous thing to say, Liv!' The indignation in his voice was palatable. 'I need all the practice I can get.'

I knew what he was doing but I didn't care. I walked right into his trap. I kissed him again and it was wonderful.

But I could only distract myself so long. I knew what I needed to do. 'I know that soon everyone and everything will be dead,' I said. 'I know it shouldn't matter. I just don't like to think that I chickened out. I want to die without regrets. I'm ready. Let's go.'

Shine reached for my hand. 'I'll be with you, Liv.'

Before we could go anywhere, I had an idea. 'Wait a minute!' I ran up the stairs and started tearing apart my room, hunting through all my carefully arranged mess.

'What are you looking for?' Shine asked.

I disrupted one of my semi-clean clothes piles on the floor. Where on earth was it?

'Liv?'

'Look at my hands!' I held them up to show him.

Shine studied them carefully. 'They look about right to me. Or did you want more fingers? Ten on each hand work?'

'No, Shine, I mean the nails.'

'Are you talking about how ragged and uneven they are? I've been thinking about it but I didn't want to say anything. Can you believe I kept that to myself?'

'No, Shine, I didn't mean that.' I wanted to be angry but I could see how proud he was and I just adored him. 'My nails aren't painted because Bex always used to insist on painting them. I wanted to paint hers one last time. I have exactly one bottle of nail polish and I can't find it.' I sighed. 'To be honest it's probably gone all gloopy by now anyway.'

'What colour do you want?'

'Well, it's sort of an off-red, if you can imagine that. Look, it doesn't matter. Let's just go.'

'No, if you could pick any colour, what would you choose?'

'Something happy. Maybe like a yellowy-orange.'

Shine reached into his mysterious black robe and brought out the happiest yellowy-orange nail polish you've ever seen. 'This shade is called bumblebee. I like bumblebees. Of course, they're all going to die today too.'

'Shine…'

'I know. I probably didn't need to mention the bit about all the bees dying. It was too sad. I heard it as I said it.'

'No, actually, I was going to ask you where it came from. It's perfect.'

'Oh.' He leaned forward and kissed me softly. 'Magic,' he said.

The good days

The history of Liv and Bex

When people heard about Bex and my dad, they always assumed he went first. That was the only way they could make sense of it. There needed to be a reason. It couldn't have just come out of nowhere. People as brilliant, bright and beautiful as Rebecca Waller didn't just wake up one day and decide it was all over. Because if that happened, and they couldn't see it coming, then no one was safe. She was happy. Wasn't she? Always smiling. A successful doctor. Always laughing. Loved by her patients. Loved by her family and friends. So in love with Paul. She was so happy. Happy people didn't just decide to die.

Bex did.

There was no inciting incident. Nothing to push her over the edge. She didn't even leave a note. That's how it goes sometimes. I'll never really know what went through her head. I think she had just been trying for so long that she couldn't do it anymore.

And so it was that on the 31st August 2023 Rebecca Olivia Waller, beloved wife, daughter, friend, and sister, tried to take her own life. I won't tell you exactly how she did it. That's the least important thing about this story. It's the least important thing about her.

Paul was the one to find her. He was both too late and too early. He called an ambulance and they managed to bring her back. The doctors were optimistic. At first they thought she was lucky that he came home when he did.

But she didn't wake up. And when she continued not to wake up, Paul had a decision to make. He couldn't do it. He didn't think he *should* do it. He gave it to us, me and my dad, the people who had loved her longest. Even when there were two of us, we were so lost. It went undecided. I think we both knew what was right but neither of us was brave enough. This was our Bex we were talking about.

Three months after Bex's attempted suicide, I got another call. It was my dad's girlfriend, Gloria.

'Sweetie, I've got some bad news.'

I knew what was coming. She could barely get the words out. She'd loved him, had Gloria. I'd only met her once before what happened to Bex. I never thought she'd stick around through all the grief and heart ache. She surprised me. People do that sometimes. She was my dad's rock. I didn't have a rock. I think she would have been mine too, if I'd let her. I thought of Bex's friend Katie at the hospital, mascara all round her eyes. *If there's anything you need, Liv. Anything at all...* I wonder how many people would have been my rock if I'd just let them in.

It turned out there was a particularly insidious heart condition that ran in the family. My grandad wasn't smote by god after all. As for my dad, there was nothing that anyone could have done. He was dead before Gloria found him. The doctors thought that the stress of what had happened to Bex might have accelerated his condition.

I could go into more detail. I could describe to you what it feels like to have your whole world come apart. How it was that I was suddenly so absolutely and completely alone. How complicated my feelings towards Bex were. How I was angry at her sometimes, for herself and for dad. For taking my whole family from me. But I don't want to remember them that way. So, instead, let me tell you about their last really good days.

For my dad, that was about a month before what happened to Bex. He had been dating Gloria for almost a year but he had been nervous to introduce us. She was his first something serious since mum, and he was deathly afraid of us getting payback for all the times he'd threatened to interrogate (and in Bex's cases actually had interrogated) our boyfriends.

Finally, Bex had strong armed him into taking us all out for a meal.

'What do you think she'll be like?' I asked Bex on the way into the restaurant.

Bex shrugged. 'I'm just in it for the free food,' she said. She didn't mean it. She'd planned this meal within an inch of its life. And she was practically quivering with excitement.

'Whatever she's like, we're going to like her, right?' I asked.

'Of course, Livvy!'

We'd been waiting for over twenty years for our dad to introduce us to a woman. There was no way we were going to ruin it for him.

I'm not sure what Bex's first impression of her was. I thought she looked a bit too posh. Her hair was long, dark and sleek. She had the kind of nails that could only have been achieved professionally. I didn't even want to look at my hands. Bex had painted my nails red but, as always, she'd done some of them with her left hand and there were little bits all over my fingers. Gloria was wearing a smart black dress, a blazer and high-heels. Her bag looked like it cost more than my car.

My dad spotted us and pointed in our direction. Gloria looked up and smiled. I knew then that I was going to love her. It was a Bex sort of smile, big, unguarded, delighted.

'Bex! Liv!' she called as if she'd known us for years. And, when we got close enough, she pulled us into a big hug. I could barely breathe. I was being smothered by her chest and the faint scent of perfume. It was quite nice. 'I've been wanting t' meet you for months,' she said in a broad Yorkshire accent. 'But this fella said there'd be nowt worse than us bonding and then us breaking up over summat daft and you girls being sad. I telled 'im we wasn't gonna break up but would he listen?'

'No?' I guessed and she beamed at me.

As the evening drew on, we ate and drank and laughed together. Gloria was everything. She was funny, warm, kind. She was divorced with a son around our age, but she hadn't wanted to bring him tonight. 'Tonight is about you,' she said.

I kept thinking that, in all these years alone, my dad had just been waiting for her. The whole meal he was leaning back in his chair, watching us getting along like a house on fire.

Somewhere into dessert, Bex suddenly sat up straight. 'Sorry, sorry,' she said. 'We've been having so much fun that I almost forgot the most important part.' She narrowed her eyes, leaned across the table and said, 'What are your intentions with our dad?'

Dad seemed to shrink into the chair. If he'd been Shine, I think he would have actually merged with it. Gloria tilted her head back and roared with laughter. 'I knew you was gonna ask that.' She looked at my dad and he nodded. 'Your dad didn't want us meeting until he were sure, and now we're both sure. This is it for us. It's me and him until the end.' She gave his hand a little squeeze, one of those tiny micro-affections that show just how right two people are for each other.

'That's so...' I began but was interrupted by Bex throwing herself across the table and into Gloria's arms. Glasses went flying everywhere. She got some sticky toffee pudding on her knee.

'Not again!' wailed a waiter. The poor lamb was only about seventeen. He looked like he might be about to cry. I dropped to my knees and tried to help him clean up. He met my eyes under the table and said, 'I hate this job.'

'I hate my job too,' was the only thing I could think to say. This seemed to help and we nodded at one another in solidarity.

All the while, Bex was snuggling into Gloria saying, 'I'm so happy for you. You're the best. You're really the best and most lovely and I need to know where you get your nails done. I'm not good at doing mine and I keep forgetting I'm a bit rich now and can afford to just pay someone for it.' My dad was watching them with the biggest smile on his face.

170.

Later, when we'd paid and I'd made Bex give the waiter half her monthly salary as a tip, we were walking back to the car together. My dad put his arms about all of our shoulders and said, 'All my best girls, together at last.' And that was it. That was his last really great moment.

Bex's was even simpler. It was about three days before she did it. She was just back from her Wiccan coven. Paul looked up over his shoulder. 'Good meeting, love?'

'Oh yes,' said Bex, her eyes shining. 'Bella's been having some trouble with a fox that keeps getting in through her window and then screaming all night. Which would be fine, but her baby isn't a big fan of sharing her cot with a wild animal and then she starts screaming too. Then the baby ends up being really stinky and it's all a big thing. Bells can't just shut the window because the fox has figured out how to open it. So, the other day we performed a protection spell on her house. But then a few of the ladies got a bit worried that the fox was seeking the warmth of the cot for a reason. Like maybe it needs shelter. So tonight we staged a stake out for the fox so that we could perform a protection spell on it too.'

Paul grinned. 'Did it work?'

'Too soon to tell.'

'What about the protection spell you did on the house the other day.'

'Well, the fox is still getting into the house but the baby has stopped crying when it does. In fact, she screams for it during the day. Her first word, at only nine months of age, is "Fox."' She wrinkled her nose. 'Well, it's something that sounds like "fox" but it sounds a bit more like something else, unfortunately.'

Paul laughed his heart out. Bex leaned down to kiss him and he held up his hand. 'Someone had thrown away some particularly potent rotten eggs today. I've showered seventeen times and I still can't get the smell off.'

'Like I care about that,' she said and dived under his hand to give him a big smooch. Then she cuddled up in his arms. 'Just so you know, if we have any kids, we are not letting them sleep with wild animals.'

'Why not?' asked Paul.

'Because of all the health risks.'

'Oh, fair enough. But what do you mean "if"? I told you we're having twelve, didn't I?'

Bex shuddered. 'I don't want to be pregnant twelve times.'

'You won't have to be. It's only six sets of twins. Or four sets of triplets. Or two sets of sextuplets.'

'Paul!'

He laughed again but then he nudged her shoulder. 'I'm only teasing. You can be pregnant no times if you like.'

'I thought you wanted kids?'

'I do, but I want you to be happy more.'

There were many big things in Bex's life. But it was these little moments that brought her real happiness. It was looking at her husband. His perfectly handsome face. Those eyelashes that had made her swoon from the first time they met. The faint aroma of rotten eggs drifting off him. And knowing that she was what he needed exactly as she was.

That's how I like to remember her. Happy. In love. Enough for him. Because, even with what she did to herself at the end, even with how angry that made me sometimes, she was always, *always* enough for me too.

Sunday – The decision

The final hours of Rebecca Olivia Waller – Sheffield, UK

'You're terrible at this,' Shine observed.

'I know.'

'You're getting little bits all over her fingers.'

'I'm very well aware.'

'And I'm not sure that "bumblebee" is Bex's colour.'

'It looks awful on her, doesn't it?'

'As awful as anything can look on someone as lovely as your sister.'

I finally looked up at him. Only, it turned out he was far too close to me and we butted heads. 'Ow! Have you got extra bones in your forehead?'

'I told you, didn't I? I'm a hyper-vertebrate.'

'Well your hyper vertebrae really hurt me.'

'Poor Liv.' He said and he kissed me on the forehead. I'd never really bought into the whole "kissing it better" thing before. Even as a child, I saw it for the poorly concealed trick that it was. But Shine's kisses had the benefit of warmth and it did ease the pain. 'You know that it wasn't my vertebrae that hurt you, don't you?'

'Yes, I know.'

'Good, because my vertebrae are in my spine and I didn't want you to think I was like weirdly floating above you or something. I was just leaning in really close so that I could hear you breathing, like a normal person.'

I turned back to the nail polish just in time to see a big drop of yellow falling on my sister's hand. 'Oh dear.' I tried to wipe it away but it only smeared.

'Oh, no! How do we fix this? What if there was some kind of remover that can get rid of nail polish? Let me do research.'

'It's ok,' I said. 'This is payback for all the little drops she got on me over the years.'

'Excellent point. Besides, she'll never know. Oh, I probably shouldn't have said that. The last thing you need on your last day on earth is to think about how your sister has no brain activity. Oh, I definitely shouldn't have said that either. Are you ok, Liv?'

But I felt myself smiling in that mischievous way Bex always did. 'This is exactly the kind of thing she would have done to me.'

A few minutes later, I took a step back and admired my handywork. Her hands were a mess. Really a mess. We're talking baby eating spag bol mess. But, even surrounded by wires and machines, she was so beautiful. 'Do you really think she was unhappy her whole life?' I didn't want to know the answer but I needed to.

Shine floated behind me and wrapped his arms about my waist. 'I think, like all of you marvellous creatures, she was many things.'

I still hesitated. 'Do you know this is what I fear more than dying?'

Shine nodded. 'Of course I do. You fear living without her.' He brushed his lips across my cheek. My skin tingled with the warmth of it. 'It's only for a little while, Liv.'

I opened my mouth to say that wasn't comforting but I found it was. We'd been apart for a few minutes in the beginning. We could be apart for a few minutes at the end. 'How do you think we go about turning off all these machiney thingies?' I asked. 'Do we call someone? No, that's stupid. If there are any doctors here they'll be with…' I stopped myself short of saying "real patients." 'I guess I'll do it.'

'I can do it for you. If you need me to.'

'It should be me.' I took a step towards her and then back again. 'Maybe a few more minutes?'

He held out his hands. 'Do you want to paint my nails?'

'Are you sure? You saw what I did to Bex.'

'Absolutely. But…' He reached into his robe and drew out another bottle. 'Please not bumblebee. I have been thinking about all their tiny deaths for the last hour and I can't take it anymore.'

'I think black nail polish on guys is kind of hot anyway,' I admitted as I began work on one of his hands.

'So does this mean you find me hot?'

'What do you think?'

'I think "yes" but I'd like confirmation, if that's ok?'

'Yes, Shine. I think you're hot. For the record, I thought you were hot before the black nail polish.'

Two pinpoints of red formed on Shine's cheeks. Black flecks spectacled his fingers.

'Is this really how you want to spend your last living hours?' I asked. 'You could be anywhere in the world with anyone.'

'Absolutely! There's nowhere I'd rather be.'

I looked up into his eyes, which were a fire red now. I saw he meant it. 'Me too,' I said.

When I was done, Shine flew about the room in circles, admiring himself.

I approached Bex's bed again. I touched the tube that went into her throat. I listened to the gentle beeping of the machines. She looked so fragile. I was scared to touch her. I knew I couldn't hurt her now. 'I don't know what to do,' I breathed. 'I don't know how to... I can't.'

Then Shine was in front of me, his hands gripping my upper arms. Holding me in place. 'Is this what you want? What you really want? To let her go.'

I thought about Bex. I thought of her laughing and dancing and sky diving. 'Yes. Definitely.'

'Then I'll do it.'

'No! It should be me. She's my sister. I should be the one to…'

'It's ok, Liv. You've done so much. Let me do this. Let me take care of her now at the end. Lean on me.'

And I did, with my whole body.

'I didn't mean literally, but this is nice.' He gave it a few seconds before he propped me up again. 'Leave the room. I'll call you back when I'm done.'

'But…'

'She won't be gone right away. There'll be time. You'll come back and she won't have any of these tubes anymore. It's better this way.'

Shine was right. It was better this way. When I returned to the room, there was just Bex. No air being forced into her lungs. Just Bex, looking like she was asleep. Just Bex, so beautiful. So much more beautiful than anyone I'd ever known.

'What happens now?' I asked.

'We wait,' said Shine. And so we did.

178.

But not in silence. Bex lived for another forty-five minutes, with me sat at her bedside, holding her hand, telling her about all the things I'd done. About all the people I'd met at the end. About how Paul was doing. About Shine and how much he'd helped me.

And then, when I ran out of my own life, I moved back to hers.

'Do you remember when you held my hand in the womb? I was just chilling in my own little amniotic sac and then you reached in and gripped onto me? No? To be honest I don't remember it either but I always loved when dad told us that story. He was so excited. And I was so proud of you.

'Do you remember when you tried to swim the English Channel when you were eleven and dad had to rescue you in a little rubber dingy and then the RNLI had to rescue you both in a lifeboat?

'Do you remember that week we rescued a stray dog but actually it was the neighbour's dog? You'd stolen it from their garden because you were worried they weren't feeding it properly since it always golloped up the treats you gave it. It wasn't starving, of course. It was just a normal labrador, but how were you to know that? The dog had the time of its life eating all those chicken nuggets and the neighbours tried to sue dad for the gastric bypass it needed to have.

'Do you remember the time you stole a bottle of vodka from daddy and got drunk with your friends? Only dad had outfoxed you and replaced it with water. You weren't actually drunk at all. And when he told you, you doubled down on it, acting goofier than ever and daddy just laughed and laughed.

'Do you remember when Paul thought that guy was hitting on you and very politely told him you were married and then it turned out the guy was hitting on him? He was so flattered that he led him on terribly and got his number. You accused him of adultery, just joking I think. He said, "It's not my fault if I'm a catch" and the way you looked at him when you said, "You really are" made me almost want to find love myself.

'Do you remember how daddy used to read us bedtime stories with all the voices? Every night before mum left and every night after too. It was the one thing that didn't change.

'Do you remember how much daddy loved us? Say "hi" from me, Bexy. I'll be there soon.

'Do you remember how much I love you? I love you, Bexy. I love you. I forgive you.'

Now I'm not saying those words killed my sister. It was probably just a coincidence that that was the exact moment that Bex's heart stopped beating.

I thought that this part was going to be hard. I didn't think I'd be able to handle it. Maybe it would have been under different circumstances. But here, in the end of days, I felt almost euphoric. Everything that was Bex was crashing about me. All these little pieces of her. Bex crying in the pillow fort. Bex doing her initiation ceremony for the Church of the Flying Spaghetti Monster. Bex dancing with me at her wedding. Bex and dad cuddled up on the sofa, reading a book. Bex singing karaoke in a way that made someone next to me in the bar say, 'I never thought someone who looked like her would sound like *that*.' Bex holding my hand when I was sad. That was Bex. This quiet, empty thing in the hospital bed hadn't been Bex at all.

Now she was free.

Still, my sister was dead, so I did cry a bit. Actually, I cried a lot. Most of it with my face buried against her unmoving chest, dripping snot all over her.

I don't know how long I cried for. It was long enough that Shine eventually said, 'Liv?'

I looked up at him, sniffing and rubbing my eyes. 'Sorry. I didn't mean to be a bother.'

'You're never a bother, Liv. Never!' He sounded so serious that I smiled. 'Do you remember how I said I wasn't allowed an opinion on things?'

'How could I forget? You nearly had a panic attack when you realised that you didn't approve of racism.'

'The thing is, I do have opinions actually.'

I laughed softly. 'I guessed.'

'I have them all the time. And I shouldn't but I'm going to tell you one. My opinion is that I wish some people didn't have to die.' He spoke the words in a hushed tone as if it was some big secret.

I got to my feet, still holding Bex's hand. 'Thank you,' I said quietly. 'But I should have done this a long time ago.'

'I wasn't talking about her,' he said. 'I *am* sorry about your sister, but I was thinking about you. It's nearly time, Liv.'

And that was when the Earth's tannoy system activated for the final time.

182.

Sunday – The end

The final minutes of everyone – Every city, every country, Earth

'Hello, earthlings. Good news, we've found a cure! None of you have to die.' There was a ripple of joyous murmurs about the hospital. Then Luna burst out laughing and said, 'Sorry, a little bit of gallows humour for you there. If you didn't get the joke, it's funny because it's not true. You are all, in fact, still going to die. There is no cure and we're not even looking for one anymore. You have just thirty minutes left. So eat your final meals. Kiss your loved ones. And pray to whatever god you believe in. It's been a pleasure hosting your final days. You really are a tenacious little species. We had to shoot down over twenty spaceships and one hundred and sixty-three missiles.'

According to Shine, at this point Max Smith shouted, 'Luxembourg, now!'

There was a pause and then, 'Make that one hundred and sixty-four missiles. That's a new record for a primitive world! You should be very proud of yourselves for trying *so* hard. See you in the afterlife, if there is one!' The tannoy clicked off.

I looked at Shine. 'Well, I guess…'

There was a crackle of static as the tannoy clicked back on again. 'Oh, and I almost forgot to mention! On behalf of the Government of the Known-Universe, we would like to formally pardon Max Smith, Representative of Earth. You may not have fulfilled your promises to us, but we've decided not to prosecute you for it since you are about to die. Go in peace, Max Smith!'

Apparently Max didn't take this well. If he had to die, he at least wanted it to be special.

'Nearly the end,' I said to Shine. 'You can be honest with me. Was it really random? The people you picked.'

'Why do you ask that?'

'They were all so *good*. So, was it random? Or were you trying to restore my faith in humanity?'

I thought Shine was about to answer me for a second but then he said, 'What do you think?'

A week ago, I would have said definitely not. He must have cheated. Chosen good, happy, hopeful people. Here at the end, I smiled. 'I suppose it doesn't matter.' I looked at my sister. 'I think you cheated at least once.'

He smiled back. 'I might have nudged the selector a little. Only once, I promise.'

'Thank you. Really, thank you, Shine.'

184.

His eyes were blue, like the ocean. They filled with golden tears.

I stepped towards him. 'Don't be sad. I'm not sad. You gave me everything I needed. Tell me something. Tell me as much as you can, as much as you know about what happened at the end. I want to know.'

And so he did. He started with the bad, what there was of it. Other than the twenty spacecrafts lost to the futility of trying to destroy the Government of the Known-Universe, there were some people who thought this was a hoax and spent their final days trying to convince others they were right. There were some who used the end of the world as an excuse to give in to the worst sides of their humanity. Wars waged in the name of religion to ensure access to holy places at the end.

But, there was so much more good than bad. So many more people living their very best lives in the end of days. So many beautiful last moments of wonderfully ordinary people.

My boss Carole Brown was curled up on the bed with her husband and her three children. She was reading to them. James and the Giant Peach. None of the children were young enough to be in the target audience. That was irrelevant. They were all quiet, listening to her voice. None of them cried.

They knew it was the end but it had been so long since they all read a book together.

Henrietta Williams was sitting in her living room with her birds. 'What do?' asked Judy, the African grey. She tilted her head to look at Henrietta.

'We're going to see other mommy,' said Henrietta, just a little sadly.

'My mommies are gay!' Judy shouted happily.

'Yes,' said Henrietta. 'Yes, they are.' She scratched the bird's head. 'And so proud of it.'

Kim Sang Heon was alone in the sky. He had no passengers. Everyone was safely off-boarded wherever in the world they wanted to be. He had done all the good he could do. Now he was where he belonged. Just him and the sky. Somewhere around twenty-thousand feet he made a decision. The aliens weren't taking him. He was going to die the way he lived, with his wings. He put the plane into a steep climb, saw his airspeed indicator rolling back. The plane juddered. He listened to the stick shaker warning. The sky rushed past as he lost altitude. He nosed the plane over further.

He could pull up now. He could save it from the stall. He'd done it a million times in training. He did nothing. A few minutes left until the end of the Earth. The mountains grew closer and closer. 'Terrain! Pull up!' The plane sang. 'Terrain! Pull up!' He lifted his eyes to the sky. His sky. 'Can't catch me, motherf-ers,' he said. Then it collided with the mountain. He won his race to the end.

Julian Ngaio was standing at the peak of Mount Taranaki with his three large brothers. He had expected to make this final hike alone, but his brothers weren't having any of that. He had tried to explain that it didn't feel like overcoming a fear if he had help. They said that was nonsense. You could be brave and still have support. Now they were sitting, all looking at him with pride on their faces. One of them loudly wooped for him. Julian had his arms wide open. The wind rushed through his hair. He was laughing like a mad man. 'No fear!' he shouted. 'No fear!'

Amandeep Singh had an arm looped about his wife Tavleen's waist. His son was fighting with a cousin over who got the best identical portion of curry. Padma aunty stared out across the room and said, 'It's been a wonderful thing having you all as family.' There was a general murmur of agreement.

'I love you,' Tavleen said. 'I wish we had more time. I wish they'd given us more time.'

Amandeep saw the beautiful blaze in her eyes and, one last time, he fell in love with her a little bit more than he had been the day before. 'No regrets, my love,' he said. 'We can't have regrets. I got to love you until the end.'

Amandeep Singh's last act on earth was to kiss his son's head and whisper, 'My favourite boy,' into his hair.

Maria Micaela Brondino was still dancing. She was crying too. She never wanted to die so young, but the music thudded through her final minutes and so she danced. She did love to dance. 'How long is left?' she called to the room.

'One minute,' came the frightened reply.

So little time. She wiped the tears from her cheeks. 'When it gets to ten seconds, let's count down and pretend its New Year,' she suggested.

'And this will definitely count as a power cut so find someone to kiss in the afterlife!' called someone else.

It felt like too soon before they were shouting, 'Ten, nine, eight, seven…' Mica looked about her. Her eyes rested on the boy she'd wanted since childhood. Then she shook her head. She'd kiss him in the afterlife. She reached for the hands of her closest friends. As the world exploded, they were spinning round in a circle and laughing too hard to count.

Bex's Paul was sitting in his parents' living room, watching a quiz show, just as he said he would. His dad was laughing at one of the answers a contestant gave. 'Cretin! Everyone knows that's King Kamonteng Ansi Inthrabodinthrathit of Thailand.'

188.

There was a photo of Bex on the table. It had been taken on their wedding day. She looked radiant, beaming at the camera. Paul's eyes fell to her and they went soft. His Bex. His one true love. He kissed his fingertips and pressed them against her face. His mum saw the gesture and smiled, 'We're coming now,' she told the photo. 'We're coming to you, beautiful girl.'

As for me, I was where I had been my whole life, at Bex's side. But it wasn't just me and her. I had Shine too. I was in his arms, warm against his chest.

I felt myself draw a sharp gasp of air. 'I'm scared,' I startled myself by saying. 'I don't want to die. I really don't want to die.'

'You don't need to be,' said Shine softly. 'I'm here.'

'Aren't you scared too?'

'I have seen many worlds end.'

'You mean your people.'

'Right, my people.' But there was no conviction in his words. Then, as if to prove my point, he said, 'This is the bit I'm good at.'

'What's going on Shine?' I thought about the way everyone else had been afraid of him or treated him with reverence. I remembered the way he had called himself a hyper-vertebrate. 'Are you the grim reaper or something?'

He cursed. 'You weren't meant to figure that out until after.'

'After what? After we die?' I tried to pull out of his arms to look at him but he held me in place. 'Shine?'

'Stay here. Just let me hold you.'

'I want to look at you.'

'Please, Liv. I don't want you to see me.'

'Why not?'

'You won't think I'm beautiful anymore.'

'Let me decide that.' He reluctantly let me go and I studied him. He was a little more skeletal than before, and he was carrying a scythe now. Even though he looked like something out of a nightmare, my heart still pounded in my chest in a way it didn't for anyone else. I smiled at him and he smiled back.

'It's strange isn't it,' I said. 'I'm terrified but I feel so brave too.'

'Nothing makes people more hopeful than knowing the end is close,' said Shine. 'Isn't there something so lovely about everyone feeling hopeful and happy and scared all at the same time? It's one of the best bits of the job.'

Trust Shine to find the beauty in death. Although, I suppose he'd be quite miserable if he couldn't. 'Just so you know,' I said. 'I don't care you're almost certainly the grim reaper. You've been my favourite part of the end. You're still the most beautiful thing I've ever seen.'

He leant his forehead against mine. His skin was cooler now. 'And you, Olivia Rebecca Waller, have been my favourite part of all the worlds.'

There would have been times in my life when I would have questioned that. How could a being who had seen so much like me best of all. But there was clarity at the end. The why didn't matter. What mattered was what I felt. And I felt happy, and scared, and sad, and alive all at once.

There were seconds, not minutes, left now. 'Is there really an afterlife?' I asked. 'Where are we going?'

The last thing he said to me before the world ended was, 'Let's wait and see, shall we?'

And, as everything went bright and then dark, I was kissing the grim reaper on the lips.

Thank you so much for supporting me and my work by reading Liv at the End of the World. If you enjoyed it, please leave a review on Amazon, Goodreads, or your preferred review site.

Also by this author

Six of Jo's seven siblings are also called Jo(e), but she's the only one who's dead.

Jo Who Died is a mother's life story told by her daughter from beyond the grave, and intertwined with the investigation into Jo's death.

A funny, sad and heartfelt story of found family, watchful crows, and a dog who does what he wants.

Kind to Crows follows Maggie Pye as she develops agoraphobia and joins a society of loveable crow enthusiasts following an attack by her ex.

Acknowledgements

For this book, more than for any other so far, I owe a huge debt of gratitude to everyone involved. For some reason, I decided I could publish two books within a couple of weeks of each other. I was right but at the expense of my own sanity and, most likely, the sanity of the people who helped me. It didn't help that the other one was a 600 page fantasy.

So, firstly, as always, my thanks go to my fiancé, Einar Ekrem, who proofread both books over the course of two days. Who renamed a (quite evil) alien species the Eih-Nor. And who declared this his favourite all time book (technically he said his favourite book of mine, but we all know I'm his favourite author). I love you, I appreciate you and my books wouldn't be the same without you.

Secondly, to Emmalene Thomas, my close friend and proofreader who I actually forgot to give a hard deadline to until a week before I needed her corrections. Thank you for rallying and still managing to finish on time. For lending me your dog's name, Luna, so I could name a heartless alien after her. For finding all the little flaws in my work, and for letting yourself get swept up enough that you cried until hay fever stung your eyes. (Also sorry about the hay fever stinging your eyes).

To my sister, Vicky, for soldiering through and proofreading both books while sick, and busy doing important law stuff. For inspiring the girl in the gig who summons mosh pits, and for briefly living in New Zealand so that I know how they feel about possums. And, of course, for the glorious "LAST DAYS OF EARTH" artwork, with the cutest little possum around, and the best artistic representation of Greece ever seen. It's such a fun drawing and fits the vibe of the book perfectly.

And to the rest of my family, my parents Ian and Jackie, and my brother, Chris. For supporting me and encouraging me to read and travel, so that I could completely accurately document what the world would be like in an alien apocalypse

And, lastly, thank you to Anne-Lise Ekrem. For being the first person to proofread this book. For making me feel special by telling me you haven't finished a book in years until you started reading mine, and for the heartwarming final comment you left in the file. You are the best future mother-in-law I could ask for.

About the Author

K. H. Walters, Author on Facebook

khwalters_author on Instagram

@kathywrites37 on TikTok

Email: kathywalterswrites@gmail.com

K. H. Walters grew up in Rotherham, South Yorkshire. She has now settled in Newcastle with her Norwegian fiancé, Einar, and her dog, Samwise. She would spend the end of the world with her family and friends, playing board games, yelling at people on quiz shows, and frantically writing as much as possible.

Printed in Dunstable, United Kingdom